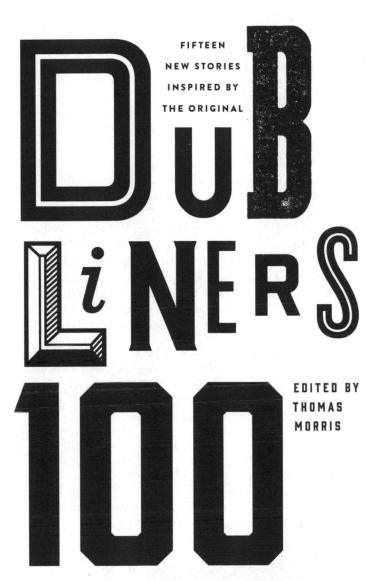

FIFTEEN
NEW STORIES
INSPIRED BY
THE ORIGINAL

DUB
LiNeRS
100

EDITED BY
THOMAS
MORRIS

TRAMPPRESS

First published June 2014 by
Tramp Press
Dublin
www.tramppress.com

5 7 9 10 8 6 4

ISBN 978-0-9928170-15

Tramp Press receives financial assistance from
the Arts Council and Dublin City Council

Thank you for supporting independent publishing.

Set in 12.5pt on 16pt Joanna by Marsha Swan
Printed by GraphyCems in Spain

Contents

Strange Traffic:
An Introduction of Sorts

Thomas Morris

1.

I have no right to be editing this anthology.

I am not Irish. I am not a Joycean academic. And at a recent wedding dinner I had to be told, in a behind-the-hand hush, that I was using the wrong spoon for my soup.

The latter mightn't seem all that relevant, but approaching an introduction to *Dubliners* – even this quasi-version of it – it's easy to feel like a child sitting at a very high table, with a delicious, over-brimming broth in front of them, armed with only too small a spoon.

2.

At nineteen I moved from my hometown of Caerphilly, South Wales to Dublin to study English literature.

I had no connection with the city other than a notion, somehow transmitted to me at sixteen, that I wanted an Irish wife. I had googled 'Ireland' + 'university', clicked the first link, and requested a prospectus. Three years later, I found myself moving to Rathmines.

Three years and a day later, washing the pint off my shirt, I learned to keep the 'Irish wife plan' to myself.

3.

The first module on my English literature degree was something called 'Writing Ireland' and one of the first texts was Joyce's *Dubliners*.

'You have to be Irish to get it,' I was told on the tram into class one day. It was rush-hour, we were standing. 'Actually,' the classmate boomed – this guy always boomed – 'you have to be from Dublin.'

I nodded.

'Oh, I've heard that,' I said sadly, my Welsh accent gleaming in my ears.

It all made sense now. I had started reading *Dubliners* a few weeks before moving to Ireland, but I hadn't felt I understood the stories. The blue Wordsworth edition I owned contained such small text – and *so* much text – on each tall page, that the stories felt like a chore to me.

And now, standing there on the tram, I understood why. I wasn't Irish, I wasn't from Dublin.

4.

The idea was simple: fifteen contemporary Irish authors 'covering' the fifteen original stories of *Dubliners* to mark the collection's centenary. In my own reading experiences, 're-written tales' tend to be dull affairs – stories that don't stand on their own legs, whose energies are only derived from other people's engines.

And I was thinking about this when I heard a Grafton Street busker butcher Jeff Buckley's 'Hallelujah' – itself a transcendental cover of the Leonard Cohen song – a cover that seems to speak to and speak past the original.

Thinking of Jeff Buckley's song – the heights its reaches, the depths it plummets – the seemingly nebulous idea of 'covering' a story came to me. It can work in music, I thought. And Joyce's prose is, we're always told, so musical …

5.

Author: What exactly do you mean by 'cover'?

Me: Um, to tell the story again, but in your own voice.

Author: Like a contemporary version?

Me: Um, if you want. But not necessarily. You're free to take the story wherever you like. Maybe even re-write it from another character's perspective.

Author: Like a re-written tale, you mean?

Me: Um, like a cover. Like you find in music.

Author: But these are stories.

Me: I know, but …

This conversation never happened. I asked the authors to 'cover' the stories in whatever way they saw fit. They easily, absurdly, accepted the idea and went with it – wherever their firing minds took them.

6.

As the tram jerked its way towards town, the classmate continued. He told me that short stories were inferior to novels, and novels were inferior to essays.

'Dickens should never have written *Oliver Twist*,' he said. 'If he really wanted social change, he should have written a political tract.'

'Yeah, I've heard people say that,' I said quietly. The boy's voice boomed so clearly I assumed he couldn't be wrong about anything.

'Another thing,' he added, 'I've noticed you don't pronounce your words properly. It's *hurd* not *heered*.'

An elderly man sat in a wheelchair near us, beside the door. He smiled at me intermittently, and cast his eyes upwards, letting me know that my gut feeling was right – *this guy really was a …*

I returned a smile, and thought of my family back home in Wales. I pictured all our movements, like dots progressing across a map. My mother would be driving to work now, my brother would be on the train, and my sister already at her desk. And I, because of some irrational whim of wanting an Irish wife, was here on a tram, in Dublin, being told I couldn't speak properly.

The ride into town that day was bumpy. The Luas seemed to jerk in spits of twenty yards. A woman – the elderly man's daughter, I presume – stood behind him, gripping onto the wheelchair's handles for support. When we arrived at Harcourt Street, the elderly man and his daughter disembarked.

Then, through the very same sliding door, a man in his thirties, pushing a little girl in a pram, got on.

He stood in the same spot as the woman had only a moment before.

The little girl, in her pram, sat in the same spot as the now-departed old man.

7.

'A strange traffic,' is how Anthony Burgess describes the relationship between the living and the dead in Dubliners. The two states, he says, seem to co-exist, walk past each other, rough up against one another, refuse to solely inhabit their allotted plots of land.

'The Dead', of course, is the example that comes immediately to mind, but there are so many instances of this 'strange traffic' in Dubliners. From 'The Sisters' where the dead body of Father Flynn literally inhabits the space of the living room – to 'A Painful Case' where Mrs Sinico's death is, for James Duffy, haunted by the life he denied her – the living and the dead move through the collection in tandem, sometimes dancing, sometimes colliding on a one-way street.

And this collection of cover versions is another act of strange traffic. Living Irish authors in communion with the dearly departed Joyce, co-existing, their stories brushing up beside each other.

Like passengers in his sidecar, the fifteen authors here have traversed the same roads as Joyce – thematically, emotionally, sometimes literally – and felt the same bends, the potholes, the dips, the rough ground. They've taken in the periphery views, the landscapes, and the characters, and re-drawn the roadmaps in their own hands.

Or, to reach for a less arduous metaphor: they've sung Joyce's songs in their own voices.

8.

The booming boy was, of course, wrong. You don't have to be Irish to 'get' *Dubliners*. Literature would be pretty banal if that were how it worked. There's no denying that your understanding of the texts can be deepened with knowledge and experiences of the locations and societies Joyce is depicting – but the stories stand alone.

Likewise, being familiar with the original versions of these stories will grant you access to nuances, to the finest and most interesting of nooks and crannies. And reading these new stories will undoubtedly diffract the loveliest of lights across Joyce's own work, offering new readings and entry points into the originals (they could even be read as creative essays on Joyce's stories).

But – and this is crucial – the fifteen stories here stand alone.

Out on the road, as spectacular vehicles in their own right.

9.

The Luas took off from Harcourt Street and railed its way towards Stephen's Green. I watched the man place his hands on the pram, as the woman before him had placed hers on the wheelchair.

Then the driver tooted the horn – three sharp bursts. The tram came to a halt. A sudden lurch. The signal lights must have failed. And as the booming boy rambled on beside me, I looked out the window as a chaos of pedestrians, cyclists, and cars veered over the tracks and the road, from left to right – and right to left – corner to corner, all moving with their own secret purposes, all beginning at different points and ending God-knows-where.

Viewed from above, I bet it looked sublime.

10.

I have no doubt that some of the authors felt when writing these stories as I did in my first few weeks in Dublin – and as I still feel this minute – small-spooned, not right for the task, too far from home.

Indeed, to 'take on' Joyce is an audacious task. But writing is not a competitive sport, and the authors haven't 'taken on' anybody. They have read, they have listened, and they have written.

And what we, the readers, have been given is a gift.

The Sisters

Patrick McCabe

There was no hope for him this time: it was the third stroke.

T he consensus was absolute – it was the worst chimney fire the town had seen in years. Already a considerable number of residents (there were thirteen houses in all), clad only in their nightclothes, had arranged themselves in anxious conclave along the front of the humble redbrick terrace, unanimously decrying the fire brigade's quite deplorable delay.

—Of all times for this to happen, I overheard someone observe ruefully, Christmas.

—It sure is a pity, sighed another broodily, turning his head from side to side.

One might have been forgiven for assuming that many present apprehended themselves as attending a major sporting event – the races, perhaps, or a football final. One individual in particular – a man in his fifties – standing not very far away from me, tapped a finger against his upper lip, frowning severely while delivering a stream of opinions in an impressively assertive voice. He was certain, he emphasised, that if the brigade didn't appear within the next few minutes then, unhappily, the McCooey quarters would be comprehensively gutted. Without a doubt, he added as a coda. Little more than a shell, you'll find, he concluded, with a candour that almost seemed rehearsed to me.

—I don't like to say it but I have to accept that you are probably right, concurred another, tubbier man, tapping the plaid toe of his carpet slipper on the gravel.

My closest friend was standing directly beside me – Douglas Greenan. Or at least that had been his name until relatively recently – when, 'on account of the telly' as he'd explained, he had decided irrevocably to rechristen himself Virgil Tracy – a notable character from the children's series *International Rescue*, in which a secret organisation of military-style puppets had pledged to make the earth a better place by comprehensively ridding it of subterfuge and suffering.

—This world, you know, Desie, behind everything, it's full of sadness, Douglas attested, I am sorry to have to tell you that but it's true as I am sure, like all of us, you will one day discover.

Being three years younger – Douglas was fourteen – I accepted that I had little choice but to acknowledge the veracity of this statement.

—But you and me we'll make it happy, won't we? I heard him suggest then with no small hint of melancholy. —You and me and the *International Rescue* team.

That was just fine by me, I assured him.

—Especially now that it's Christmas, he said, abstractedly fingering his plastic triangular IR badge.

He had sent away for it in *The Hornet*, a funny paper to which we both subscribed.

—But none of us here will have to worry, the tubby man was saying with a smile of near-triumph illuminating his countenance, for all of us have been through chimney fires before – and worse. And one thing you can say is that we've always come through! As indeed we should – for this place means everything. It's part of us. It is us.

*

Beneath the streetlamp where a sooty cloud idled dolefully inches above the power cables, the coloured glass sphere of an eight-vane catseye rolled from the slope of Douglas's thumb careering in a trail of light towards the neat circle we'd described in the hard clay. We did that almost every day now – had done ever since we'd become close friends.

—Marbles are go! you would often hear Douglas peal, and you better watch out, for Virgil Tracy he gonna sweep the boards!

I hoped he did. I'd have given Douglas my entire collection if he'd asked, being as he was my friend – the best I'd ever known.

These were my thoughts when Jimmy Keenan happened along, knotting the cord of his dressing gown as the gravel crunched beneath his unlaced boots, biting on an Afton cigarette and agreeing with everyone that things had begun to look very bad indeed.

Jimmy worked as a supervisor on the railway – you'd see him going by with a pencil tucked behind his ear, whistling. He often engaged me in conversation. Addressing me as Spokeshave – by virtue of my reputation for learning, or so I'd assumed. Only recently I'd captured yet another much-coveted essay prize in the school for my response to the suggested title: Our Community and What it Means to Me, an account which saw our schoolmaster, after a protracted period of perusal, professing himself pleased with my 'Herculean' efforts, in the process citing a German word Heimat, with which until then I had been entirely unfamiliar.

—In a sense it means home, the castle in a person's heart, if you will, he told the class, but in truth there is no specific English translation. However, Desmond's composition appears not only to have understood the concept but described it with an eloquence and intensity of feeling I find quite extraordinary … Which is why I am awarding you, boy, first prize. Congratulations!

In terms of human happiness, there was but one day that could compare with it – which had occurred some years previously, a night where there had been no chimney fires, one other Christmas Eve when Santa had provided me with a little scarlet-jacketed dragoon made of tin, complete with bayoneted rifle and tall shiny bearskin hat.

I'd kept him close for most of that year but had somehow, bafflingly, mislaid him and remained inconsolable for an unbearable length of time. Only for Douglas I don't know what I'd have done.

At least we've got our marbles, he would soothingly suggest, and if you would like I'll gladly lend you my IR badge. Then he would give me that reassuring smile, which seemed the repository of all the world's contentment, agile and eager, genuine and bright – but also steady and fixed, like the pole star – entirely at odds with the profusion of sparks now capering ferally amongst the swaying electric wires.

—But then it would come as no surprise that you'd be a scholar, Jimmy Keenan was murmuring, for Spokeshave is exactly what we all used to call your Dad in our time – aye, after Shakespeare the bard of Stratford, do you see. Boys but he had the brains, your father. Ah the world, I mind him saying this day in fourth class, this lonely place where we arrive like shadows only to find ourselves already preparing to depart. You're a ringer for him, young McCooey, so you are – and that's a fact. It might as well be your Dad standing there. Beneath the stars, watching them jumping sparks.

I was profoundly gratified by this revelation. But not, I regret to say, by the sight that was soon to meet my eyes.

Mrs Lavery and her maid Bridie had appeared without announcement or ceremony and were standing directly in front of me, frowning in their corded candlewick dressing gowns. Bridie kept wagging her finger as she spoke, erupting sporadically into episodes of what seemed faltering and unnecessarily clandestine laughter.

Some moments later they were joined by the genial, bluff, general handyman Pat Corgs. Pat often weeded Nurse Connolly's garden. When they inquired as to her absence, her habitual inquisitiveness being well known, they were told that no, she wouldn't be in a position to come out and have a look. Because she wasn't, he whispered, angling his tousled head, in the best of health. Indeed, he continued, with his brows knitting ominously, the truth was that he feared the worst.

He had heard her the previous day, he elaborated, when he had been going past the house, rasping pitifully behind the front room's heavily draped window where her nephew had arranged a little camp bed for her beside the fire.

—I felt sorry for her – in there in the sitting room all alone, racking the way she was, desperate hoarse don't you know. Bad, aye.

This world which she entered like a shadow, I thought. But couldn't – not even privately – bring myself to complete the sentence.

All of her children were abroad, I knew, with her nephew being the only relative remaining in our little town. I wondered where they all might be – and what they might be doing now.

Pat was leaning against a tree. He mopped his brow with a freckle-blotched forearm, observing the small dark sputniks wheeling in slow arcs at an immense height.

Douglas appeared to have forgotten all about the smoke and the fire – which for me seemed to have become a bat-winged creature temporarily obliterating the face of the moon. He narrowed one eye and flicked the transparent catseye. A dull crack followed and marbles went scurrying like insects beyond the depressed circumference.

For the briefest of moments, it seemed as though it wasn't Douglas Greenan at all – or Virgil Tracy from International Rescue either. It appeared as though in that briefest of instants he had been taken away, never to return. The prospect truly horrified me – the thought of having my truest friend replaced, for even the most infinitesimal period.

I swallowed hard and covered my eyes. Before a startling cry sharply splintered the air and Bridie and her maid both went hurtling forward simultaneously, standing transfixed with twin forefingers extended upwards.

—O in the name of God would you look at that! O may the good Lord Jesus come to our aid now!

Misshapen swirling penumbral whorls were simultaneously bloating lengthways and vertically, before dissipating and vanishing like rags that had been angrily torn. They seemed to me as id-creatures then – (whose essential essence had recently been comprehensively catalogued in the pages of The Hornet) – with their talons craned above every inch of the black-scarred brick of the terrace. We have come to darken your town, they seemed to say – or rather to suggest without ever speaking, stealing effortlessly into your mind, locating there recesses as formidably colourless and forbidding as themselves.

The smell was becoming close to unbearable. It was sharp and acrid, stingingly choking and perhaps if Bridie had not cried out the way she did maybe no one would have become agitated. But she had, however – and as a consequence some of the children began sobbing a little.

—If the fire brigade doesn't come soon – what will we do? This is the worst chimney fire ever – it's the worst fire of all! Why did it have to happen at Christmas – why? Please can anyone answer me that!

The children, not unreasonably, were concerned that the season of glad tidings had now been interrupted – perhaps even worse, irrevocably ruined. Perhaps they were thinking of melting rubber dolls, I thought to myself, or crooked malfunctioning clockwork toys. In spite of myself, I was at loss as to know why I persisted in entertaining such a variety of dread possibilities. To compound matters, my face had grown unbearably hot. I could see Jimmy Keenan smiling at my father, who by now had appeared in his shirt sleeves at the open doorway. He said nothing – as Jimmy Keenan folded his arms, flicking away his Afton cigarette as he turned to Pat Corgs and said, with a shake of his head:

—Did you ever see smoke, in your life, that could compare?

Pat low-whistled and didn't say anything – but there could be no doubting the concurrence, which was firm and respectful, almost awed in the presence of an authority greater than his own. He folded his hands and lowered his head. The way he might have done at, say, Nurse Connolly's funeral.

—In a competition for chimney fires, Jimmy continued, for smoke that comes out of chimneys – whether at Christmas or any time of the year – I'd have to, on reflection, give it a nine.

I marvelled at their pride and composure as both men stood there in steadfast combination, as though on the point of elevating numbered cards.

*

Terence Bly was an amateur photographer who once upon a time – or so he claimed – had published a print in the Roving Eye section of the popular newspaper, The Irish Press. And although he liked to insinuate that he was a 'snapper' much in demand, this was the only indication of any only real achievement in that field. He arrived up bustling, appraising the proceedings and framing the tableau like a true professional. He stroked his chin and studiously remarked:

—Most extraordinary!

In what respect he chose not to say, continuing to pace the gravel in circles, before wheeling with alarming suddenness as though on the verge of casting a wide tarpaulin in an attempt to snare the recalcitrant crimson inferno leapfrogging jaggedly across the rooftop slates, some of which had already begun fragmenting. Events were rapidly approaching crisis point. Of that there was no doubt in his mind, Pat Corgs declared as a bell of saliva appeared between Jimmy Keenan's lips.

—I seen chimney fires. In my time, I seen plenty. I remember when Josie Quigley's house near burnt down. But, bad as it was, Terence, it was nothing like this. If you want my honest opinion, I would have to say that already that most of the guts of that chimney there is gone.

A seam of silver contained the bead of saliva temporarily – and then it was gone, falling for what seemed an age in the gloom. I watched as Mrs Lavery achingly wrung her hands.

—It's just that … she began.

—Yes? urged Pat.

—Even if it wasn't Christmas Eve. It still would have spoilt it all on the childer.

—Of course it would, agreed Pat.

Bridie stared reproachfully at the rusted sixpence of the moon. Then she found some shreds of tissues in her pocket and gave them her attention, to no apparent purpose.

—Because it's that time of year when everyone prefers to forget all their troubles, she continued, and go back in their own minds to those trouble-free days of childhood.

—Ah do you mind them, sighed Pat, those days without a care, sometimes it used to be like you were living in a storybook.

—*The Little Match Girl.* That was one the nuns used to read us. I wonder do you remember that one, Pat? sighed Mrs Lavery, as she added, My Daddy, God rest him, he always loved that one.

—Jesus Mary o fuck by the living Christ! shrieked Jimmy Keenan, stumbling backwards, crooking his arm over his face as he did so, clearly in anticipation of a blowout. But nothing happened.

—She used to see visions, elaborated Mrs Lavery, inside the fire like that one up there.

An amber cloud suddenly bulged before sundering.

—My favourite story about Christmas was – yes, *The Little Tin Soldier!* squealed Bridie, reacting as though astonished to hear herself speak the words. Mrs Lavery cast her a disapproving look, as though she had flagrantly traduced protocol by not requesting permission.

—Aye he was good, agreed Jimmy Keenan, as a matter of fact my young lad likes nothing better than to read.

—He jumped into the fire, didn't he? interjected Pat, wasn't that what happened, fired himself intill the smoke and perished? Was that …

Jimmy gripped him fiercely by the arm.

—Look out there Pat, for the love of God! Because I think that guttering's going to tumble!

He actually pushed Pat Corgs out of the way, as it transpired, for no reason at all. For, as it transpired, no portion of the guttering was seen to dislodge itself.

—Do you hear me, I'm an eejit! laughed Jimmy, pushing you out of the way like that! An eejit is what I am!

Subsequently a few brief moments of levity ensued as Pat suggested to his companion that, considering these developments, he might reasonably consider himself a member of the much-admired contemporary comedy troupe The Three Stooges.

—The way you're going on, pushing me out of the way like that, you boy you Keenan!

—I'm a card! laughed Jimmy, I'm worse than Larry or Curly or Mo so I am!

I looked up to see my father standing belligerently in shirtsleeves in the doorway, as though about to take on all-comers, with squared fists striking the attitude of a bareknuckle boxer. However, he seemed confused, hesitating awkwardly, being washed by the moonlight before swinging around to return inside.

That was when it happened – when I felt myself becoming out-of-sorts, as though my body were being inexplicably, unaccountably filled with a heavy viscous liquid, tilting sideways, before I found myself becoming quite elated – and it was as though we were all of us now present at a carnival where a magnificent fireworks display had somehow miraculously just been mounted – and where, far from being shadows, my neighbours now were bathed in a phantasmagorical mercury-silver light. And just for a fleeting moment it really seemed quite wonderful, before I returned to myself – untilted, ossified.

On the far side of the back door, I heard something splinter shrilly, perhaps a cup, maybe a glass.

—I told you didn't I, I heard my father bawl, I warned you not to pile up the papers. What do you think is going to happen if you stuff a grate? A dozen times I warned you that inevitably they'd catch. But naw, you wouldn't listen. Not that that should be a surprise. For when did you ever listen? Did anyone ever hear of a McClarkey who'd ever listened?

Mrs Lavery yawned, swivelling her eyeballs towards Bridie, tapping her mouth with her open hand. Her maid smiled, sidling up beside me and placing a soft feminine hand upon my shoulder.

—What are you getting for Christmas, Desmond? she inquired.

The question had taken me entirely by surprise. Which was why I responded: —A little tin soldier, perhaps.

Even though I was getting no such thing. Chairs were were being violently hurled around inside. I heard the back door flap and crash.

—The bloody thing's been rotten since the cursed day we rented this place! Why in Christ's name could you not fucking listen to me, piling up your rubbish and papers, not even bothering to clean the thing out. And to top it all now the bloody fire brigade is late!

I looked over at Douglas, still turning the transparent sphere between his finger and thumb, with its orange whorl resting sideways inside. Which, without warning, seemed to wilfully break its confines and sweep across my face like an overwhelming dawn-coloured wave.

Bridie was tugging her ringpull up and down. I prayed she'd stop.

—Bitch. For that's what you are! I heard my father snarl.

—No, you said, it'll do for a while yet. There's no need, Benny, to have it swept. And now what've you done? You've gone and disgraced us in front of the whole town.

—We're not disgraced, she protested, it's just a chimney fire, Benny.

—Don't you dare contradict me, don't tell me there isn't smoke when I can see it with my own eyes!

—I'm not saying there isn't smoke. I didn't say, Benny, that the kitchen wasn't full of smoke. In fact I'm not talking about smoke at all!

—Fuck you and smoke!

A small plea for clemency went nowhere as a dull blow sounded. Soft and sickening, just as though a cushion were being plumped.

I heard Bridie murmuring to Mrs Lavery, avoiding my eyes.

—But he's right, all the same, Mrs, in a way what he's saying it really is the truth. I always make sure not to pile up too much papers. You can't be too careful. Could go up like a torch, you know. Any chimney – up like a torch. O Lord God above would you look at that smoke.

It might have been a troupe of dwarf-dancers rehearsing, climbing from the pots to arrange themselves in pairs, indistinguishable in their bluish-greyness from the shade of the slates, commencing yet another frustrating, contemptuous variation – a kind of bitter ghost-tango, I thought, between unresting spirits returned to avenge.

I caught Mrs Lavery frowning quizzically:

—Is it dear, would you say, to get a chimney swept now?

Bridie was emphatic, shaking her head as she doggedly tugged the silver ringpull of her nylon housecoat.

Zzzzipp!

I shuddered involuntarily at the sound – I couldn't determine why. Its static suddeness, perhaps.

—O not at all, the maid continued, doesn't Pop Brady do it, Mrs, for only five shillings. He was telling me only recently that he's bought himself a whole new set of brushes.

—Mm, is that right? Is that a fact do you tell me now? Well then, isn't it just a great pity that they never thought to call him in time. Ah well – these things happen, I suppose.

She coughed politely before laying a firm but gentle hand on Bridie's arm.

—It's just that, you see – well, anything could happen. I mean, all I'd be afraid of is that it might catch and burn us all. Burn the whole row, if you see what I'm saying.

Bridie nodded, in fulsome agreement.

—Every house in the lane could go, she said.

—That's what I'd be more afraid of than anything! Mrs Lavery suggested through lips that seemed barely in existence at all.

—And it'd be just an awful tragedy, if it happened at Christmas!

—It doesn't even bear thinking about, Bridie. Just think if it did – what I mean to say is if it had happened an hour or so later, when all of us – when we were all in our beds …

—Little kiddies, fathers, mothers. Jesus, Mary – the whole lot of us!

—Lying there in bed, dreaming about Christmas. All those lovely Yuletide things …

—The Little Match Girl.

—The Little Tin Soldier.

—And Christmas pudding topped, as always, with a little sprig of holly. That's what we'd be thinking about.

—So sad if it were to happen like that!

—I mind The Three Stooges in a film, Pat Corgs interrupted – Disaster At Xmas I think it it was called. Went and set the whole house on fire! Maybe you should have been in that picture, Jimmy, you that's as bad as Curly or Larry – or even Moe!

Jimmy laughed, waving away the good-natured jibe. However, Mrs Lavery's expression still remained grave.

—It would just be heartbreaking if that were to happen, she

continued, with the risk of all the children being burnt alive there in their beds. Choked by the smoke – they say it can happen in a matter of seconds.

A gleam appeared in the corner of Bridie's eye as she swallowed.

—God between us and all harm, she gasped, the poor wee childer never waking up. They say that it swells up in your throat like a fist.

—Like a fist made of smoke.

—And that's how you choke.

—A fist in your mouth.

—So you can't even scream.

—Not being even fit to cry or scream.

—Until you are lying there, silent –

—Not fit to utter a word.

—Not fit to utter so much as a word –

—Lying there, your throat choked with smoke …

—Dead.

—She appears to be slowing a bit now, Jimmy Keenan suggested.

—This is definitely one for *The Irish Press!* Terence Bly suddenly declared, parting his legs as he elevated the camera. —Before it dies down!

I looked up to see my father standing in the concrete yard, stiff and livid but his face as white as the moon at his shoulder. He didn't say anything as he picked up the shovel, abstractedly scraping some ash into a small mound as he crouched. I heard Bridie heave as at last her hands seemed to find her pockets, a benign maternal grin beginning the process – with immense effort, it seemed – of evening itself out as she heaved a sigh of relief.

—Well doesn't it just go to show, she said, after all the talk it didn't take so long in the end! Isn't God good? Because I really do think that we're out of danger! Look – the smoke! It's almost completely gone so it is!

Mrs Lavery nodded, enjoying a luxurious, however brief, little shiver as she suggested:

—Sure what was it anyway only a bit of an auld chimney fire!

Jimmy Keenan pulled an Afton packet out of his inside pocket, closing one eye as he retrieved a small butt. Pat Corgs was laughing at what they called 'the good of it all!'

—You'd look well, chortled Jimmy, getting yourself excited about a chimney fire! Something that happens every day of the week!

—A wee bit of smoke – I mean who cares or gives a damn!

—Not me anyway! chortled Jimmy, enjoying a long luxurious drag of smoke.

—Now you said it! A chimney fire – you'd be a lucky man if that's all you had to worry about, wouldn't you?

—Correct and right! chirped Terence, shouldering his shiny black Polaroid bag as though on the point of dashing to the airport. As he slid his thumb beneath the leather strap he announced:

—All I care about is my snaps and I've got them! Irish Press here we come, for The Roving Eye has gone and done it again!

And off he went briskly, turning the corner to – only to find himself almost run over by the fire engine.

—Right! Which number are we looking at? the chief fire officer demanded impatiently, disembarking.

—Ha ha ha I'm afraid youse are too late! laughed Pat Corgs, the whole thing's over bar the shouting – hardly even so much as a smidgin left!

—A smidgin of what – what are you talking about? the fireman countered with unconcealed irascibility.

—Smoke! returned Pat, it's gone and made a cod of youse so it has!

—Youse are worse than The Three Stooges, snickered Jimmy Keenan, it's the fire brigade who ought to be acting in Disaster At Xmas!

Everyone laughed at that – with a mounting inclination towards dispersal becoming manifest. As an image lifted noiselessly in the charred weighted air I thought again of the little match girl and the smoke from her quenched tinders greedily consumed by the universe's maw, abandoning in its wake the tiniest of quavering, sunset-coloured glows – which from that vertiginous absence might have been anything – the jacket of a discarded toy dragoon, perhaps, or even a marble. Or, though I bitterly joined battle with such a possibility, the dimming embers of a diminished fastness, the once unbreachable ramparts of home.

An Encounter

Mary Morrissy

It was Joe Dillon who introduced the Wild West to us.

The idea of writing to Ardmore Studios is yours; you want to be taken on as a film extra. You love the felted intimacy of the picture house, the great elsewhereness of the images. You have just seen *Love Story* and have a crush on Ryan O'Neal, though you don't admit that, not even to yourself. You imagine – but can't quite believe – that in a hangar in Co. Wicklow you might rub shoulders with film stars, and be discovered.

'Discovered?' Jo queries. Jo Dillon is your best friend. She is thin and fierce. She has a frizzy mane of ginger hair that bundles on her shoulder like the brushy tail of a fox. You, on the other hand, are stout – that is what aunts call you. At school, you are Fatty.

'Well, *Ryan's Daughter* was filmed in Dingle and they used locals,' you argue, 'so we could do crowd scenes.'

'Serving girls,' Jo says, warming to the idea, 'or wenches, maybe?'

You tell no one, not your mother, or Jo's parents. Jo comes from a small damp house in Highfield Cottages where they sleep two to a bed. You have more room at home but different shortcomings. Your father's a Customs man and he's just been put on Border duty, which means that he'll be away for months on end. Your mother tells you he'll be staying in rooms in Dundalk, even at weekends. And maybe permanently, she says. You don't know if that's a threat or a way of telling you something. So you don't want to be troubling her about Ardmore. Anyway, it's your secret, yours and Jo's, not just from parents, but from the other girls in school, prettier, more popular girls who would mock you for having notions.

You write the letter to Ardmore because your handwriting is neater. All through August you watch the postman's movements waiting for a reply. But you are back at school before it comes; it's the end of October and the answer is no. Come back at eighteen, the studio manager writes. That is four years away, an age! Jo is cross when you tell her you've been rejected. She demands you bring the letter to school, as if you are trying to deceive her.

'Now what,' she says, sighing, thrusting the letter back at you. Everything with Jo – even her disappointment – contains a demand.

The promise that has tantalised you both all summer fizzles out. When you cycle home from school together, as you do every day, you are flat with one another. The petty rivalries of the convent day keep you going as you pass the Ardtona stores, where sometimes you stop to buy sweets, and the British army houses, as you call them, a long row of pretty red-bricks with louvred shutters; some have trellises outside with rambling roses climbing up them like an illustration of Ye Olde England on a biscuit tin. But by the time you reach the Dropping Well hill, your conversation has petered out.

Usually, you dismount here; your mother calls after you every morning – no cycling down the Dropping Well. It is a steep hill plunging down to Classon's Bridge over the Dodder. A girl in your school, Hetty Gardner, was killed when the brake cable on her bike snapped as she hurtled down this hill at speed; she went over the handlebars and her head was stoved in on the bridge's stone balustrade. Every time you pass the spot you remember Hetty Gardner though she was several years ahead of you and you didn't know her.

But still, it is a milestone. It means you know someone who's dead. Hetty Gardner serves as a warning of what can happen to a careless girl who goes against instructions. Disobedience can be lethal; that's the lesson.

You get off, as usual, at the crest of the hill but Jo sails rights past you, just like Hetty, coat and hair streaming as she freewheels down the forbidden slope and over the bridge at the bottom. She is putting it up to you. Your friendship is like that; you are practising on one another for the later wiles of love. But you are not going to get yourself killed cycling down the Dropping Well hill for Jo's sake. Your mother is an honorary widow and there are responsibilities when you're an only child that Jo can't understand. She is the eldest of five sisters. You have seen her at home, how she can command a mood with a disconcerting glare. Her mother is often in bed – trouble with her nerves – so Jo has half-raised her sisters and they always kow-tow to her. There are times when you're a bit afraid of her. She is travelling so fast now that once she crosses the bridge and turns left, her momentum keeps her going halfway up Milltown hill. She has got as far as the Dartry Dye Works before you catch up with her.

'Scaredy cat!' she says, like you used to say to one another in primary school. But now it's full of venom. Sometimes you wonder if she likes you at all. But she waited for you; that must mean something. She has propped her bike up against the wall of the dye works. It's a building that looks like a Carnegie library or a town hall, with a clock tower, though the clock has never told the right time. She stands with her arms folded, still waiting but there's a kind of menace attached to it now, as if she's daring you to say something.

'It's very dangerous what you did,' you say.

'I don't want to hear any of your goody-goody talk,' she says and taps her foot impatiently on the ground. You know it is your move; you feel a row brewing and you don't like it. In Jo's house there are operatic arguments, all the sisters shrieking at once, and the mother trying to keep the peace. In your house there's just you and your mother and the ghost of a better Daddy.

From somewhere down below you hear the sound of the river burbling over stones. A laneway winds down by the dye works. Shoals of leaves have gathered in the gutter in crisp, ochre pools.

'I wonder what's behind this place,' you say. 'Just think, we cycle by it every day and we've never explored it.'

You push your bicycle ahead, past a dirty-looking building with a toothy roof, a mill of some kind, and a couple of crooked-looking cottages whose walls seem to belly out on to the lane.

'Are you coming?' you ask, using Jo's tone back at her.

Out of sight of the road, the lane opens into a flat low sward of sweet green grass. You and Jo throw your bikes down. The river is shallow here and you step down on to a kind of rubbled shore. The water is fast-moving, brown and brackish. It eddies noisily when it meets an obstacle – a tree root, a boulder.

Although you are close to home, none of the familiar landmarks of your everyday journey are visible from here – the Dropping Well hill, the Dodder bridge, the Nine Arches viaduct. It is like you have passed into another country. Jo skims a few stones. She has tomboyish talents you envy.

The day is damp and misty, the sombre sky heavy with bronze-bellied clouds. You notice the plastic bags snagged on the bare branches of the bushes on the opposite bank and the milky traces of effluent from the mills staining the water. You feel your false sense of leadership deserting you.

'Let's go upriver,' you offer, remembering the phrase from your history books. Dr Livingstone, I presume.

Truculently, Jo follows. Pushing the bikes, you take the narrow path by the river's edge that bends into the gathering dusk. It is over-hung with trees that arch and cringe. Underfoot is a light skim of leaves. The river is tamer now. There is a footbridge up ahead and when you reach it, you and Jo without saying anything, stop, drop the bikes on the path and climb the steps to look down at the river from above. There is something mesmerising about the still water, bloated with the sky's reflection. You feel yourself falling in time, back to a day spent with your father, oh years ago, when you were small. He took you to his office in Dublin Castle and left you in a brown linoleum chamber with a long window while he ran an errand. You were sitting in a bentwood chair which your father said not to stir from for any reason. He'd be back very shortly, he said. There was no clock in the room – and even if there had been, you hadn't yet mastered the second hand. As the time ticked on in your head, you became afraid that he'd forgotten about you and that you would be left forever in this bleak and empty room, waiting. The door opened once and a man with a hat asked what your name was. When you told him, he asked you where your daddy was.

'Left you on your ownsome, has he?' the man wheedled, kneeling down beside you and chucking your chin. Then he rose unsteadily and left, shutting the door behind him. You were sure he would go and fetch your father but no, another age passed before, finally, the door opened again. Your father came in as if he'd only been gone a few minutes and said he was all yours now. He took you down to the river and you walked along the quays to get the bus home.

'The whiffy Liffey,' he said. 'Want to see?'

He lifted you up so you could look over the quay wall. Maybe it was the way he grabbed you suddenly and swung you high in his arms, and then leaned out perilously over the water, that made you see clearly what he had in mind.

'Don't Daddy,' you wailed. 'Don't throw me in, please, don't throw me in …'

You began to beat him around the shoulders and face, your cries getting louder as he struggled against you. A lady in a headscarf intervened, asking your father if everything was alright with the little girl. Perfectly, he said, and landed you roughly on your feet.

'That's the last time I'll bring that child anywhere,' he told your mother. 'She made a holy show of me.'

'Did she put a stop to your gallop?' was all your mother said.

Don't throw me in, Daddy, please don't throw me in …

'I'm bored,' Jo says.

In the distance there's the sound of rushing water.

'Hear that?' You want to shake off your own mood.

You return to the overhanging path and follow it again until a sharp turn in the river brings you to a waterfall. A heron stands perched, one-legged, in mid-stream.

'Look, just like Niagara Falls,' Jo says.

It's the first time she has sounded impressed. There is a railing on the river side of the path and beyond it a concrete platform. You both climb over the rail and go to the edge of the platform and sit down, dangling your legs over the water. The noise and the spray hitting your faces returns you both to your old exhilaration and for a couple of moments you and Jo are perfectly happy, disappointments forgotten. It is then you see the figure of a man approaching. You both stiffen, all the warnings of your mothers coming home to roost. You have strayed off the path. Despite the hectic truckling of the water, it seems suddenly very quiet. Jo springs to her feet and makes for the railing. She steps on to the bottom rung and stands on it, her arms on the top rail bearing her weight, like someone on the prow of a ship. You are slower to react; your gabardine coat hampers you as you clamber up to standing, trying not to show too much leg or any underwear.

'Oh feck it, Una,' Jo cries out, 'he's a flasher, he's a dirty old man!'

She heaves herself over the railing, darting in front of the man, and flees to her flung-down bicycle. The bell on the handlebars makes a feeble chime as she rights it. She stands facing him on the path. She flicks one of the pedals as if she might charge him.

'Come on,' she shouts to you, 'come on!'

But the stretch of cracked concrete between you seems an impossible distance to cross and the man is standing sentry at the railing between you.

'Shouldn't you girls be at school?' he says. His voice is light and thin; you expected gravel and smoke.

'Don't talk to him,' Jo shrieks.

'School is finished,' you tell him. 'We're on our way home.'

'Taken a bit of a detour, haven't you?'

You can see Jo hoiking her leg over the bar of the bicycle, gesticulating and pointing clownishly behind his back, but in all your years as friends, you've never agreed on a secret sign language.

'Your friend is leaving,' he says. 'Aren't you afraid?'

'No,' you lie as you watch Jo wobbling down the path the way you came. Soon she'll get to the bend and you'll never see her again. This is the parting of the ways. Dumbly, you will go with this man because it is easier than trying to run away or make any protest.

'Come here,' he says crooking his finger.

As you move gingerly towards him you realise that Jo has got it wrong. He is not a dirty old man at all. True, there are no laces in his shoes and his dark trousers are mossy with grease, but he isn't old. He's the same age as your Uncle Leo, the one your mother calls her baby brother. He has unkempt straw-coloured hair that falls over his forehead and curls over the collar of his coat. His face is sandy with stubble; his eyes blue and blameless. And Jo is wrong about another thing; his ashen coat is buttoned all the way down. There are no horrors on display. Not that you can see. He reminds you of the sailors your father used to talk to when he took you down the docks to get out from under your mother's feet. In his spare time he sang with a musical society and he'd taken up Italian out of interest in the arias. He used to try his Italian out on the homesick sailors. He would shout up at them from the quay as they smoked out on the deck and sometimes one of them would come down and talk to him and breathe the word 'bello' over your head.

'Let me help you,' the man says when you get to the railing.

Up close he smells of woodland rot. You place your hand in his as you clamber over and leap to the ground on the other side. He presses his lips to your knuckles and looks into your eyes, half-teasing, half-candid. Later, you will count this as your first kiss.

'Aren't you lovely,' he murmurs. No one has ever said that to you. Glancingly he grazes your cheek with the palp of his fingers. 'No marks, no blemishes.'

You feel a shiver run through you.

'Someone walking over your grave?' he asks. But you know it isn't that. He laughs, a sound snagged with phlegm.

'Have you ever seen the arch?' he asks.

You shake your head.

'It's a triumphal arch like the Arc de Triomphe. Like in Paris.'

Paris? On the Dodder? This is a trick; you know that much. Offering something exotic, a secret, to draw you away.

'I can show you,' he says.

You don't even nod to agree. It's as if the decision is already made. He will lead you off to some dark place of brambles and dirt and there will be no Paris. You will be the girl spirited away by the evil stranger, as unreachable as Hetty Gardner, known only as an object lesson of what not to do. And you don't care anymore. They say there is a point in drowning when you give up struggling, when it's easier to go down, to succumb … you have reached that point when you hear the screaming. It startles you because you're not sure for a moment if it is you making the noise. But it isn't you. It's Jo, standing at the bend in the path, her mouth a black chasm of agony. You turn to look at her and when you turn back the man is disappearing down the path away from you, his coat-tails flying, like a spooked bird. You watch until he is out of sight. And even when you can no longer see him, you can still hear him, thrashing through leaves.

'What were you thinking of?' Jo demands, a reverend mother again.

Your heart is pounding.

'You left,' you say.

'I was going for help.'

But you don't believe her. It is almost dark now and you ride home in silence, muttering your goodbyes when Jo turns off at Highfield Road and you continue your journey alone as the street lights come on.

'Where on earth have you been?' your mother demands when you get home. 'Well?'

But you can't answer because you feel you have travelled from a long distance and everything at home seems suddenly smaller and oddly safe.

A lifetime later, when your mother is long dead, your father asks you to take him for a spin by the Dodder. He's in a wheelchair so he needs help. You don't see much of him. You visit him in the home; you do your duty. He doesn't ask for much but when he does, you think it a good thing to accede, if only because your mother is no longer there to disapprove. It is the first time you have been back to this spot. Much has changed. The dye works with the clock-tower is now a crèche and the old mills have been torn down and replaced with a sleek grey facility that apes its predecessor in shape but does not belch anything unseemly into the river. See, you tell yourself, nothing to fear here. The bogeyman of your youth is unlikely to materialise in the blue sunshine of a July day. He and his ilk will be at home watching a porn channel, not ghosting around the Dodder. As you walk, pushing your father ahead of you, you realise that it is not the flasher (as you have come to call him as a kind of shorthand) you are afraid of meeting, but Jo. Something came between you after that day. Distrust, suspicion. You grew apart. Jo's mother's health got worse and the following year she was taken out of school to look after her brood. She became the missing person in your life, the one who was spirited away, leaving you behind. You think of her as you reach the waterfall. Niagara. It is no such thing, of course; it's a shallow weir.

'Will we turn back now,' you ask. 'There's nothing much after this.'

'Now, that's where you're wrong,' your father says, thumping his hands on the arm-rests of the chair. 'There's Ely's Arch, built in 1779. Once the grand entrance to Rathfarnham Castle and quite the spectacle.'

A vision of the sandy-haired young man comes to you. Thinking about him has always made you blush. But now you are smarting with the recognition of truth reaching you across the decades like the light of a defunct star.

'Is it anything like the Arc de Triomphe?' you ask.

'Well, I don't know about that,' your father says, 'but there is a resemblance ...'

You make a u-turn with the wheelchair.

'What are you doing?' your father asks. He twists his head and looks up at you. Furrowed forehead, hank of grey hair, rheumy eyes watering. You have an urge to bring him to the river bank, set the brake on the chair and leave him there. You want to go back ... get on your bicycle and pedal to Highfield Cottages, knock on the door of Number 9 in case Jo might still be there, waiting for you.

'This,' you say to your father, 'is as far as I've ever gone.'

Araby

John Boyne

North Richmond Street, being blind, was a quiet street except at the hour when the Christian Brothers' School set the boys free.

N orth Richmond Street, my aunt told me, was a quiet street until I was sent to live there. Neither she nor my uncle had wanted me with them, I knew that much, but what choice did they have when my parents left for Canada, claiming that they would send for me when they were settled. My aunt showed me the box room that was once my cousin's and told me not to get too comfortable.

Jack's room was exactly as he left it on the day he wandered into the path of a number 7 bus as it made its way around Mountjoy Square towards the Rotunda Hospital. The toys and games were a little young for me, the books were ones I'd read a few years before, but I didn't mind for I felt a longing to wrap myself in the comfort of the past. I had lived in a big house before all the trouble started, when we had money, but that was gone now. People said it was my father's fault, or at least that he bore a considerable portion of the blame, and there were those who said he should be brought back from Canada to face the courts. They said he had destroyed lives and that families would not recover for generations. I scanned my uncle's copy of The Irish Times every morning in hope that they would achieve their goal; I wanted my father brought home. And my mother too, I suppose.

It was late autumn and the nights drew in early but I preferred to be outside than stuck within those suffocating walls. The house was stale, the wallpaper peeled in corners above the cooker revealing a yellow-mottled skin behind. There was a dog who was no fun and whoever heard of such a thing as that? My aunt sat in front of the television most of the day, drinking tea and eating custard cremes, a cigarette always on the go. My uncle, a civil servant, preferred the pub after five o'clock and I didn't blame him. Occasionally they spoke to each other. A school had not been organised for me yet; they said it would come soon but the days passed and no changes happened there. I didn't mind. I yearned for company but couldn't bear the idea of having to make new friends. Boys my age intimidated me; they always had. And to be a new boy at a new school? There were few ideas more alarming.

Some afternoons, I would wander up Ballybough Road and turn right towards Fairview Park, which was big enough for me to investigate in sections. I found empty cider bottles, small black bags filled with dog shit, Sunday supplements, half-eaten sandwiches and once, a pair of women's underwear ripped asunder at the seam as if someone had removed them with violence. I saw a man crying on a bench as he read a letter, digging the nails of one hand into the palms of the other. I watched a boy and a girl kissing in a copse, his hand moving greedily beneath her shirt, and when he noticed me, the boy gave chase until I collapsed, panting on the damp grass, and let him slap me about the face a few times.

There was only one child living nearby, a girl of my age named Mangan, but it was her brother, a few years older than she who caught my eye and made me hope for a protector. He went to school in a uniform but came home most afternoons in rugby shorts, his face mud-striped and wild, the hairs on his legs clay-caked to his skin.

Every morning, I watched from my bedroom window as he left the house, yawning, his bag slung over his shoulder, his tie already loosened around his neck as he put the black buds in his ears, scrolled to the music he wanted and went on his way. Then I would charge down the stairs, out the door and run after him, glad that his music cocoon prevented him from hearing me marching along behind. If he turned he would see me, of course, but he never turned. And had he noticed me, I would have pretended not to see him at all but would have simply trotted along, ignoring him, a boy off on some piece of private business. I thought of him through the day and wondered whether he was taking notes in class, talking with his friends, changing for his match. I wondered what kind of sandwiches he ate at lunchtime and what he washed them down with.

He was on my mind constantly and it frightened me that I could think of no one else. Were boys not supposed to think of girls, had I not read that somewhere? He had thick, messy blond hair that looked as if it never saw a comb and was stocky, like rugby players often are. How old was he, sixteen perhaps? Just a boy but a man from my perspective, a few years his junior. I saw him everywhere, both awake and asleep, and knew not why. I caught sight of him in a supermarket one afternoon, a girl walking along with him, and followed him through every aisle, my eyes on their hands, hoping their fingers would never connect. I wanted him to move away, or for my parents to send for me, so that I might stop obsessing, but dreaded the notion of a For Sale sign going up across the street. I was as confused in my adoration as I was excited by it. I imagined what it would be like to be his friend, for him to hold me. He might hand one of his ear-pieces to me so we could listen to a song together, our faces close out of necessity. We would smile at each other, our bodies touching as our heads bounced in time with the music. He would reach for the ear-phone afterwards, his fingers grazing my cheek and smile at me.

The gap between his front teeth. The scratch of stubble along his chin. The coloured thread he wore around his wrist. His habit of wearing runners with his school trousers. All these things were matters that I took note of and thought about, day and night.

Once, when I woke too late to see him leave, I returned to my virgin bed in my dead cousin's room and threw myself around beneath the blanket, thrashing like a wild animal, my feet wrapping the pale sheets around my ankles, mummifying myself in their whiteness as I kicked out in self-loathing and buried my face in my pillow crying out his name, spoken with longing, then with vulgarities attached, then obscenities, until finally, spent and soiled, the sheets a disgrace, I examined my thin young body and felt as alone as I have ever felt in my life, the isolation of a boy who feels that an unfairness has been thrust upon him that he will never be able to share for who would ever understand such a thing or tell him that he is not a monster?

At last he spoke to me, asking why I never went to school. I told him there were plans in that direction but they seemed slow in coming to fruition.

'You're the lad with the father in the papers all the time, aren't you?' he asked and I nodded, embarrassed by my father's disgrace but flattered that I had some celebrity in his eyes. 'Do you play rugby at all?'

'Not yet,' I said. 'Maybe when I start school.'

'Do you watch it?'

'On the telly.'

'Sure come up some Saturday morning to the school and watch one of our matches. Half-past eleven till just before one. Lots of lads your age do. Bring us an orange for afterwards,' he added, laughing before running across the road without even a goodbye and leaving me on the banks of the Tolka River, alone and delirious. I wanted him to take more care on the roads than my poor cousin had.

Saturday morning came and my aunt said I was to stay at home until she and my uncle were back from the shops as there was a delivery that they were waiting on.

'Can they not leave it next door?' I asked and she turned, annoyed by my refusal to help, and said that she didn't want to go bothering the neighbours.

'I don't ask much of you,' she snapped. 'What use are you anyway if you won't do one simple thing after we've given you a home and food and a bed to sleep in?'

Eleven o'clock came and no sign of the man from An Post. Eleven-thirty. Twelve. I could feel my stomach turning in convulsions and once, in a fit of dramatics, I convinced myself that I was going to be sick with anxiety and hung my head over the toilet bowl. I went outside and stared anxiously up and down the street in search of the van. I marched around the house, cursing all those who worked for the postal service and banged my fist off the bedroom wall until I thought it might bruise. Finally at twelve-thirty the doorbell rang, the parcel arrived and it needed no signature at all despite what my aunt had said and I threw it on the kitchen table in a fury, grabbing the freshest looking orange I could find from the fruit bowl and ran through the streets towards the school where the brother of the Mangan girl played his rugby.

I was afraid that the match would be over by the time I got there but no, a crowd of a hundred people or more were gathered on the side-lines on all four sides of the pitch, a sea of blue and white for one team and green and gold for the other. They were cheering the lads on and I looked out for Mangan, whose back bore the number nine, and followed him with my eyes.

A girl was standing next to me with two boys and I listened in to their conversation.

'That's what I heard anyway.'

'It's not true.'

'It is! I happened at the party last Friday.'

'I heard he was into your one from St Anne's.'

'It was her was into him.'

'That's a lie.'

The girl turned and looked down at me and asked me what I thought I was doing and I blushed and made my way down the field, watching as the ball was thrown from player to player, scrums were formed, lines were drawn, throw-ins were made and tries were scored. I saw the brother of the Mangan girl take the gum shield from his mouth during a break in play and watched the way his upper lip contorted as he released it, his tongue extending for a moment before diving back inside. A line of saliva ran like a wire from his mouth to the lump of plastic in his hand and only when he turned his head to the left and spat on the ground did it disappear and I felt a groaning somewhere deep inside me. He raised his shirt a little to scratch his belly and a fine trail of dark fuzz made its way beneath his navel to within his shorts; his hand followed it in for a moment as he adjusted himself. When the whistle was blown he threw the gum shield back in his mouth and turned to run in my direction with a grace that belied his bulk, his head watching at every moment as the ball made its way above the heads of twenty boys and he reached both hands up, leapt in the air, dragged it into the pit of his stomach before hoisting it back with his right hand and throwing it further down the field to some shadow whose catch I did not even turn to see.

Soon, the game ended and there was cheering on the pitch. I gathered that Mangan's team had won but it had been a close thing and a good-tempered game for the colours intermingled and there was a clasping of fists and quick hugs, hands to the back of each others' heads.

I dared to call his name as he trotted off the pitch with one of his friends and he turned to look at me, uncertain at first before a moment of recognition made him smile.

'You made it,' he said, tousling my hair as if I was a child before running on, running past me, running away, turning to his companion and laughing about something as they disappeared back towards the changing rooms and out of my sight. I stood there as the spectators started to disperse, hoping that he might come out again. He had told me to bring him an orange and I had done so but I hadn't given it to him. He hadn't even noticed it in my hand. Finally, a group of them emerged, an excitement of boys, pink-faced and wet-haired, talking and laughing loudly, sports bags slung over their shoulders, drinking cans of Coke and devouring bars of chocolate in one or two bites. Mangan among them, at their very centre.

I waited until they were all gone and walked slowly down the driveway, making my way back towards North Richmond Street, where I had no desire to be, the orange still in my hand. I was a boy uncertain where he was going, abandoned and left wandering in a part of the city that was unfamiliar to me, a place that would take me years to understand and negotiate.

That part of me that would be driven by desire and loneliness had awoken and was planning cruelties and anguish that I could not yet imagine.

Eveline

Donal Ryan

She sat at the window watching the evening invade the avenue.

W hat good is this? Mother asks nightly, and gestures about her. What good is any of it, with nobody to share it? Oh, Augustine, she wails, my Augustine! And brandy slops from her bulbous glass onto her monstrous lap. A portrait of my father hangs apologetically above the living room fireplace; she sits at an angle from it in a hard high-backed chair and contorts her neck backwards and upwards to regard him censoriously. I nursed you through three illnesses, she says, and my reward is to be here, alone. My oil-on-canvas father avoids her eyes, preferring to gaze balefully at the crumbling cornice. She swings her eyes toward me and allows her pupils to dilate, as though to focus on me would be to acknowledge my existence, diluting her argument with my father's image.

Mother's friend Reeney organised the first Welcome Night. She booked a medium-sized conference room at the Radisson Hotel and nobody came. I think Reeney forgot to distribute her leaflets at the reception centres. Mother and Reeney and her blank-faced sisters and Reverend Black and a group of press-ganged dancers and musicians sat before a table of apple tarts and sandwiches and assorted cordials and Reeney tutted and sighed and pinked and reddened and eventually gave up and instructed the surly serving staff to clear everything away, there had obviously been some misunderstanding. Mother was ecstatic, she was replete, energised, on the drive home. The. Whole. Thing. Disastrous! Not one foreigner! How would they even have gotten out there from the city? And the shrill glee in her laugh made my eardrums vibrate.

Mother organised the second Welcome Night. In the Protestant Young Men's Association hall on Athlunkard Street. People came, of various shades. She counted and catalogued and licked her lips, almost curtseying to the more regal Africans. She unwittingly inverted people's names, addressing them by their surnames. Reeney gently, discreetly corrected her and Mother thanked her through gritted teeth. She poured tea and tepid coffee into mugs from giant flasks, and words into the embarrassed silence. She asked whether they were Christian or ... otherwise. What is otherwise? a man asked. Oh, you know, Islamic or some such, Mother replied. What is sumsuch? the man asked. I think he was ribbing her, in a playful way, but it was hard to read his face, the stony blackness of it. He reached out a massive hand for Mother's proffered tea, to stop the terrible rattling of cup against saucer, I think. He sang a keening song of long, unwavering syllables at the end of that night, and clapped and hooted wildly at our Irish dancers, and Mother declared herself his friend, and declared her night a victory. There were people there, at least. Real live refugees. That was the first night I saw Hope.

Hope travelled from France to England on the Eurostar in the summer of 2008 in a car with a man to whose friend she had given three thousand pounds. She was told she still owed seven, and would have to work it off. She travelled across England and Wales in a lorry driven by a silent man, lying on his narrow curtained bunk, and to Ireland across a stomach-churning sea, and to Dublin in the back of a white van with flowers painted on the side. When her trafficker slid the panel door back she kicked him in the testicles with all the force she could muster in her half-starved, dehydrated state. Force enough to dump him on the pavement, moaning. He sounded like a dog about to die of thirst, Hope said. Mweeeeh, mweeeeh, mweeeeh, she mimicked softly, and laughed, and looked in my eyes and through them and into the centre of me and I laughed with her. Work THAT off, she said to him, and stepped over him and ran away. I fell in love with her as she told me that story.

Evelyn. You have a girl's name, she said. I laughed and told her how as a teenager I considered my mother's naming of me to be an act of violence. My schoolmates needed no nickname for me, just a chanted elongation to keep time with their blows: E-ve-line, E-ve-line. I never fought back, just curled myself tightly on the ground. I didn't tell Hope that part. I asked my mother once why she'd called me Evelyn. Waugh, she said. The humourist. Waugh was a man, you know. Anyway, it was your father's idea. Her raised eyebrows and downturned mouth said that was an end to it; the matter was not to be raised again. She knew I knew the truth.

I told Hope I would support her application for asylum. She thanked me and told me there was no way to do so. She knew the system, it was almost the same in every European country: form-filling, refusal, appeal, refusal, deportation. Except here there is more welcome nights, yay! And she raised her arms in mock celebration and laughed and looked in past my eyes and I sat rigid, priapic, praying she wouldn't notice. Her legs stretched sweetly out from her, creamy-brown, viciously muscled. Her firm breasts strained the fabric of her light summer dress. I wondered how it would feel to be kicked in the balls by her.

I drove to Galway and scoped out hiding places; hostels and cheap hotels where cash would be unquestioningly accepted, where long-term arrangements could be easily, namelessly made. I read ads in the Advertiser, for cottages on the coast, in the mountains, in the cracked and cratered Burren. I found a renovated cottage thatched with reeds and daub on the midway of a boreen that led to a tiny sheltered bay. I doled fifty twenties into a callused hand and was thanked in Irish. I vainly searched my ancient memories for the words for *You're welcome*. I drove home filled with a feeling of lightness, of freedom, a taste in my mouth of delicious exile. Hope was sitting cross-legged, absorbing the sunlight, on the steps of the reception centre. I don't know, she said. What about your mother? I cannot love a man who will mistreat his mother.

Mother's bladder loosened itself as she climbed the stairs that evening. She made her way onwards in deliberate oblivion, leaving an acrid trail of thin wetness on the cream stair carpet. What message was there for me in that haughty pissing? She turned from the landing and her swollen cheeks were dissected by tear tracks. All of her was leaking. You go, she said, and leave me here, and you may stay gone, my fine boy. Oh, she could see me now. I had told her I was going on a speaking tour with my father's books. Ha! she said. Who would want to hear about that ... flimflam! That ... weasel's ... *pornography!* It's all arranged, I told her. Well, and a sob flew wetly from her, unarrange it. Please, Evelyn, I need you here. I almost believed her.

Hope didn't like the car I had hired. Why not a Mercedes? *Everyone* drives a Nissan. My mouth dried as I drove and no amount of water would moisten it. We need to be low-key, I explained, to meld with the background. Meld! she spat, Ha! We stopped in Spiddal for petrol and food. The counterman was gruff and regarded Hope darkly. You see, she said as we drove away, everywhere I am watched, suspected, hated. She stood still before the cottage, looking at the mottled thatch. What is this? A hut. She turned and pierced me with her eyes and I felt my desert-dry mouth open and close again soundlessly. The low wooden door was stiff; she sighed as I struggled and pushed past me, entering the dark cottage with an exaggerated stoop. She unbuttoned her coat and stood in the kitchen and said It will do.

Do you think I will let you touch me, because you have brought me here, hidden me away? Do you think I'm your slave? No, no, I whispered. I just love you. You don't have to do anything. I cooked a stir-fry and she sat silently across from me, looking past me through the window at the darkening sky. My throat constricted, my stomach clenched. My cutlery rattled against my plate. I'm sorry, I whispered. For what, she whispered back. I didn't know.

I lay that night on the broken springs of a musty sofa-bed and thought of Mother and the duty I was leaving undone. To care for her into old age, to see her to the end of her path. I imagined her lying prone and buckled at the foot of the stairs, soaked in brandy and blood. The sound of Hope's soft, long breaths floated from the bedroom. I imagined the warmth of her body, the nakedness of it, feet from me. I imagined her anger if I appeared at her bed and woke her. I imagined her softening in the sunlit morning, walking hand in hand with me through the salty breeze to the sandy cove at the end of the boreen and saying Yes, this is good, we will stay here a while. I imagined her lips on mine, our mingled breaths. I said a childish prayer and wondered if my father could see me, and what he would think of me now. If he would say Go home to your mother, you fool. Or, Well done, my son, now you're a man. What had I done, really, but fall stupidly into unrequited love and make a promise to save a woman from deportation that I couldn't possibly keep? My money would be gone inside six months. Hope thought I was rich. I let her think it. I thought of Mother at her best, laughing, calling me Ev, her blue-eyed son, before she fell to drink. Fell.

The rent for the cottage was paid for a month. I left a small bundle of notes on the trestle table before the fireplace. The heavy door, swollen from the damp air, scraped again on the threshold and shrieked as I pulled it open; Hope stirred, then appeared at the bedroom doorway, silhouetted in moonlight. My breath caught in my throat, the shape of her. She saw the money and knew I was leaving her. I set my face to the dark world outside, to the moaning wind. Evelyn, she cried behind me as I started the engine, Evie, please.

After the Race

Andrew Fox

The cars came scudding in towards Dublin, running evenly like pellets in the groove of the Naas Road.

T

he seven-minute-mile pack of the Third Annual Central Park Run for Renal Artery Stenosis squeezed through the tunnel beneath the 65th Street Transverse and bore down on the finish line. There – sandwiched between jiving Kelvin Kidney, the race mascot, and a convoy of carts selling bottled water, ice-cream bars, hotdogs, funnel cake – a crowd of family members jiggled, waving banners of encouragement and love. The runners mostly were young men from finance or the law, shoed in box-fresh sneakers and braceletted in metrics gadgetry. On their backs, the leading pair wore yellow t-shirts printed with the calligraphed logo of Binder-O'Sullivan, a name newly familiar to the bulk of the crowd, as it had become throughout the city, since senior partner Dick Binder's deposition before the SEC.

For five long and thoroughly reported days that March, a federal prosecutor had combed over the firm's involvement in a merchant bank divesture that tanked an employee benefits portfolio once valued in the high-nine figures. And although no wrongdoing was judged to have taken place, Farley and Associates, the media strategists hired to manage fall-out, had suggested a month's gardening leave in Jamaica, where Binder – at his own expense, the press release was careful to stress – currently was thinking over what he and his team had done. Farley also had initiated a number of tactics designed to rebuild what they called the firm's *reputational equity*, including the announcement both of a college scholarship fund and of a volunteer programme committed to staffing Sandy relief measures in the far Rockaways. But the strategists had been especially keen to encourage individual efforts – 'Let's *humanise* you,' they said – chief among which was Charles O'Sullivan's pledge to compete in every humanitarian race to which the city would play host over the course of the following year.

O'Sullivan, whom to Farley's delight the Post had dubbed *Charity Chuck*, was the younger by a decade of the firm's two named partners and a former track star at Yale, who only narrowly had missed the cut for the '92 Olympic team. He parted his hair in a bouffant style and had softened but never lost his Boston accent, a combination calculated to recall Kennedy, which it did for many of his clients – insurance executives mostly, with names like Moynihan and O'Keefe – who neither could deny his charisma nor quite put their finger on its source. His limbs moved now with light inevitability, his eyes' sharp focus easing as he closed on the crowd that welcomed him. Keeping pace at his elbow was Eddie Villona, a stocky associate fast making a name for himself in the trenches of litigation, whose always snarling face during his stint as an ADA had led more than one court officer to mistake him for the defendant. And bringing up the rear, with a stitch like a knife wound carving through his stomach, was James Doyle Jr, a flushed and paunchy summer associate too excited to appreciate fully how sorry a figure he cut.

In '05, James's father had ground-floored O'Sullivan and a host of other wealthy Irish-Americans in a development of luxury apartments in Dublin's docklands, then ensured in '08 that each had got away cleanly before the banks came to collect. On the proceeds of this and other ventures, Jimmy Sr had bankrolled his son at Cambridge, and was now two-thirds of the way through paying his tuition at

Dartmouth. NAMA recently had seized the guts of the old man's opera-
tion, and in Ireland he was making headlines of his own. Jail time, he
had been assured, was out of the question, but there was talk of his
having to sell the house in Dalkey against which he had guaranteed the
previous year's expenses. Nevertheless, there would be time enough to
see James through to the Bar and, now that O'Sullivan had offered the
boy a junior associateship upon graduation, to set him up in the city.

And what a city it was! On his summer salary – more money for
eleven weeks' work than his schoolteacher mother ever had made in
a year – James had rented a one-bedroom apartment in the far West
Village with a balcony and a doorman. With O'Sullivan, he had eaten
in more Michelin-starred restaurants than there were in all of Ireland;
and with Villona, he had drunk cocktails in the finest fleshpots of Soho,
where, on one occasion, he had met and gotten along famously with
a tech billionaire, and on another had chatted until dawn with an
underwear model who left him with a nine-digit cell phone number
and a story he would tell forever. Often, on such nights, James had
thought of his father, the bullying tactics to which he resorted both
as parent and as businessman, and he knew that he himself already, at
twenty-four, had a chance of achieving the life of real wealth and class
that always had remained beyond the old man's reach.

His colleagues crossed the finish line a good half-minute before
him, and as James sweated and wheezed the last few yards he watched
the two men lean into deep groin stretches, O'Sullivan waving and
smiling and looking as though he might just run the course again
for fun. On all sides, men, damp-shirted or shirtless, drew up to their
fullest heights so as to force girlfriends and wives to teeter on their
toes to kiss them. They turned their big heads stiffly and squeezed
water past their lips from bottles held at six or seven inches' distance.

'Let's go, Ireland!' Villona said with a scowl of mock irritation. 'We'll
be expecting better from you at the marathon next year, Jimmy.'

James gritted his teeth as he crossed the line and bent forward
against rising gorge. He braced his hands on his knees, too light-
headed to think of words and too out of breath to speak them.

'All I'll say is you'd better be in training,' O'Sullivan said as he tucked a complimentary towel inside his collar. 'Villona, make sure the kid gets signed up at the Club – if he makes it that far.'

The partner synced his wristband with his iPhone and led his two young colleagues to the park's perimeter wall, where he hailed a cab and directed it east towards his apartment and a fresh set of clothes. From there, James knew, he was to attend a reception at the Irish Consulate before the three reconvened later on downtown for dinner.

'Come on,' Villona said, reaching for James's elbow. 'If we don't get you to a masseuse soon, brother, you'll need a doctor.'

They crossed the street and fought through a throng of tourists towards the Athlete's Club, an Art Deco high-rise with Italianate arches that occupied a full city block. From poles above the canopied entryway hung a spotless Stars-and-Stripes and an orange-white-and-blue emblazoned with the seal of New York State. On the ground floor were a state-of-the-art gym, a half-dozen squash courts, an Olympic-sized pool and a dance studio the Bolshoi used whenever it visited Lincoln Center. They nodded at the desk clerk, who greeted them both as Sir, and went straight – Villona striding, James already limping – to the elevator bank, where Villona swiped his gold member's card to take them to the treatment suites.

In a locker room furnished with Finnish wood, they changed out of their running gear into soft white robes and slippers, then padded to a bright room with bamboo-covered walls, pan flutes on the stereo, and two women waiting by the tables to oil and knead the strain from their tired bodies. James pressed his face into the pillow as the masseuse went about her work, and an hour later, as he watched Villona rise and peel a fifty from his billfold, he thought again of his father, the innuendo that doubtless would have blighted the old man's conversation here, his urge always to haggle and his resolution never to tip. When he himself had real money, James thought, he would be both wiser and more generous with it: would invest only in sure things rather than gambling on bubbles, would think always of those worse off rather than of himself.

Unlike Jimmy Sr, who conducted most of his business from the Horseshoe bar, James had worked, he felt, for everything he had. True, the old man paid the bills, but that was all he did — and he wouldn't do for long. It was James who had put in the hours at the library while his classmates went out drinking; James who — with a sense of decorum inherited from his mother — had made lasting relationships with professors leading to an offer of a clerkship in the Seventh Circuit, which, delicately and with no hard feelings, he had managed to defer. And although it was true that his father had made the connection with O'Sullivan, it was James's own facility with the law, he was sure, that had seen him excel over the summer. And now, once he and Villona had dressed in their suits and visited the membership office, he felt glad and justified in taking his reward.

The restaurant to which the cab whisked them was a nouveau French-American place on the ground floor of a gut-renovated warehouse in Tribeca, which had topped both the *Time Out* and the *New York Magazine* summer hot-lists, and which already had a one-month backlog of requests for reservations. The three colleagues were joined, in an alcoved dining room with white-clothed tables, by Michael Roche, a visiting Irish minister, with whom O'Sullivan spoke loudly and often about his desire to visit once again the town in Laois from which his ancestors had hailed. Roche encouraged him to do so, going so far as to recommend an hotelier in the vicinity, who, he said, 'will do you a reasonable rate'. The minister had wet blue eyes, dry hair without colour, a dark suit that fit him squarely in the shoulders, and hands, James thought, bred for hurling or hod-carrying. He cut his *Mosaic of Venison* roughly with the edge of a fork, wiped his lips with a napkin and gulped, as the other men sipped at glasses of wine, from pints of beer.

'And what about you, young Master Doyle?' he said over flourless chocolate cake. 'Do you know, I know your father well? Terrible what's befallen him of late, but he'll come through yet, please God.'

'Please God,' O'Sullivan nodded.

'As will we all,' the minister said, 'please God. The Irish are a resilient people, as you, Mister O'Sullivan, know full well. We look after each other, at home and abroad. I hope you'll remember us Jimmy when you're a partner yourself or sitting up on a bench somewhere.'

'Of course,' James said, rolling the stem of his glass between his fingers.

'There's a good lad. Your father has made you well, I see. And I'm glad to say you're taking after him quite nicely.'

James drained his wine and felt his head begin to swim with it. Would he ever be free, he wondered, from such underhand goodwill? He thought of his father installed at a bar or yelling from a football touchline, shaking hands and making promises tied unbreakably to obligation.

'Let me tell you about my father,' he began, but Villona interrupted.

'To Ireland,' he said, staring hard at James, and as the other men raised their glasses a waiter appeared to deliver the bill.

'And to New York,' the minister said.

That night, the city appeared to James as one vast system of trade. With Villona and O'Sullivan, he walked the minister to his car, past restaurants and bars where men and women joined in negotiation, the clatter of voices and glasses tumbling from open windows. Limos barreled south along Greenwich, where, in the distance, James could see the jostle of lights and glass that signified the Financial District. He lit a cigarette.

'The youth,' Roche said as he climbed into the car, 'think health will be theirs forever.' He sniffed. 'So long, Charlie.'

'So long.' O'Sullivan turned to his colleagues with eyebrows raised. 'I don't know about you, gentlemen,' he continued as James watched the minister's car retreat, 'but I need a drink after that.'

The partner led the way to the door of a small hotel, through its spartan lobby to a velvet-paneled elevator and out onto a roof deck where a party was in swing. The bar, a long glass oval lit from beneath in purple neon, was scrummed around on all sides and smothered in talk. James waded into the heat of touching bodies and shouted at the bartender's back. At length he was served and, balancing three Ketles in the triangle of his splayed fingers, he turned to find himself alone.

He forced his way through the crush, suffering the stabs of elbows and the sharper sting of exclusion. A woman dancing drunkenly struck him with a trailing hand and smiled dumbly as the contents of his glasses splashed against his shirt. James set the glasses down on a ledge and drank their remnants off in quick succession, placed a cigarette between his lips but felt on his shoulder a bouncer's heavy hand.

'Sir,' the bouncer said. 'You'll have to take *that* outside.'

In the elevator, James resolved to make one final circuit and then go home. But on the pavement, speaking with a short man in a tight grey suit he recognised immediately as Norman Farley, the media strategist, he found Villona and O'Sullivan at last. He sidled up and tried and failed to join their conversation. Farley was testing a theory about Appalachian folk music and the use of homemade instruments, to which Villona, jaws set tightly, listened while watching James — appraising him, James thought.

'Jimmy!' O'Sullivan said once Farley had run out of steam. 'Our lost wanderer returns. Though a little late, alas. I reckon we're ready to cut out.'

'Okay,' James said, but the tide of Farley's talk commenced once more to swirl around him, and presently, without quite realising how, he found himself in the back of a cab speeding for the Brooklyn Bridge, the on-ramp dipping nauseatingly beneath him.

Farley's apartment was a loft at the top of an industrial building right on the water in Dumbo, with one glass wall through which James could see the entirety of New York harbor. He looked into it, and it looked back at him, a darkened mirror lit here and there by the cabin lights of pleasure craft. He could feel the building sway as though a boat at sea, then realised that it was he who swayed. Farley, at the flat screen that dominated the far wall, was demonstrating to the other two a video game that one of his clients had developed. Villona held a controller. O'Sullivan gripped a bourbon. The game was a first-person shooter in which players hunted each other through the streets of an unnamed city. Its graphics were fluid and sharp, its sound effects all boom and bludgeon.

'You're a young man, Jimmy,' Farley said with a smile as he passed James a controller. 'And a cruel motherfucker from what I've heard. You'll like this.'

'I'd just like to say —' James said, but at that moment Villona took aim from a rooftop and fizzed a sniper's bullet through his ear.

Soon, they were playing for money, Farley setting traps in abandoned textile plants and Villona charging headlong through alleyways, guns blazing. On the coffee table sat an upturned football helmet, autographed by a tight end whose sponsorship deals Farley had helped to recover following a rape allegation, into which — with each fire fight, each spray of arterial red — the men dropped crisp bills from their wallets, then crumpled bills from their pockets, then IOUs jotted on business cards and lunch receipts and scrips of paper torn from the sides of cigarette boxes.

As the night wore on, James died again and again, giddy with the size of the sum he couldn't help but lose. The final tally showed that Villona had broken even, with Farley the runaway winner. James translated into months of work and rent the money he had lost, the amount becoming suddenly and very terribly real. He knew how sorely he would regret his losses in the morning, but for now it felt good to stand beside O'Sullivan at the window. The early light picked out the city's spine as though it were a great and awful creature yet at rest. O'Sullivan tapped on the glass.

'Daybreak, gentlemen,' he said.

Two Gallants

Evelyn Conlon

The grey warm evening of August had descended upon the city and a mild warm air, a memory of summer, circulated in the streets.

I t was a fairly beautiful morning, not stunning or anything like that, but passable for September in Dublin. The usual finger-wagging mist was hanging about but there was an occasional chink in the grey, a small coquettish curtain being parted slightly to show what was up above. The sky was threatening to come out. If you had never seen continuous cerulean you would have thought the whole day alright.

Two boyos, one called Lenehan and the other Corley, turned in their beds. One of them vaguely wondered about last night and what had happened to give him this twinge of uneasiness with himself, but the turning over tumbled him happily from self-examination back into sleep.

The participants in the conference, reluctantly called *Another Look at Joyce*, collected their various bits and pieces, assembled themselves as best they could, and trooped out on to the streets of Dublin to make their ways to Trinity College. Some people knew every name of every street, others had declined that route. They were off to make sense of things through looking at writers and what they might have meant, and how the dead ones stood up or didn't. This was as good a way of making sense of the world as say business is, or prayer.

Mind you, it depends on who is leading the prayers, Ruth thought, as she got ready to ascend the steps, talking to herself quite audibly – a woman needs to be able to do that, round out her thoughts without interruption, it might be her only defense against what's in store for her. The *esprit de l'escalier* can be overrated; what you think is more important than what you say. She knew that, she'd had to fight for every inch of intelligent space as most of those around her did their very best to dirty her brain with small talk and small views of herself. She'd looked at conversations that she was being forced into and she'd seen them metamorphose into mouths that were chewing and spitting out her dreams.

Toby Doyle took the steps, sometimes two at a time, behind her. He could afford to miss the occasional one. He had just caught sight of that Ruth and wanted to almost catch up with her, he'd heard that she had new things to say. As he hurried to get closer to her, a shadow from the past walked straight at him, never ducked, straight at him, aiming to go through him. It blacked out the scrap of sun that was trying to blossom. Shivering, he steadied himself, so as not to become mesmerised by the brief bit of dark cast on the stone. At the same moment Ruth felt an invisible breath kiss her face. She touched her cheek.

The two boyos had begun their walk down the slight hill of Rutland Square, Lenehan had done his first resentful jump down off the footpath.

The delegates entered the hall, gave some mild greetings to colleagues, Ruth to Peggy and that Italian woman, Toby to Joseph and to him from Princeton. No one took offence at any noticeable lukewarmth – they were used to this level of distraction. Ruth sat down where she could see one of the few windows. A couple of drops of old rain slid down it. Toby sat on the raised seat, two rows behind her. Lachey sidled in beside him. Other delegates shuffled or bent, then sat, the occasional one jauntily threw a leg over a knee. They took out notebooks or, in the case of some, the latest iBook. A few stared straight ahead as if they were somewhere else. An awful lot was going on today, they had much to say, much to argue, rows had to be stoked and conclusions had to be hinted at. And choices had to be made as to which conflicting papers to attend. Now this was a real dilemma. It might seem harmless enough from the gods above but it was not, it was not, and required some thought, and then changing of mind after more thought. There were those who could take these decisions with humour and there were those who could not. The plenary paper of today had started. All hands got on deck, and in no time at all it was time for coffee.

'I see you're talking about the two gallants. Bit of a leap for you,' a tall, rangy man said to a corpulent one. They were surrounded by men in various shades of in-between.

'I'm going to that,' the suddenly animated Italian woman said in an olive voice. After all, she could like the way Joyce painted the men, she was in no competition with that, her way of seeing them was not much different to his. The ceiling of her own sky had maybe helped him view them. And he had liked women in his way, had the nerve of a woman in places, had what it took to face down those who were lesser than his own. He had sat at a window in Trieste, just as Lawrence had later looked out at Gargnano and carved the dirt of the mines while the diamond light of Lombardy poured from the sky around him. From Piazza Ponterosso Joyce walked Dublin, doing his best to brush aside the cataracts of nostalgia. It was while swallowing a mouthful of wine, and drawing perfect smoke into his lungs, that Lenehan and Corley jumped out at him on the street corner of either city and said *go on, sharpen your nib, write us then if you're so good. They surprised him really, he'd been thinking of how dry the sun here seemed, when all of a sudden he saw Corley sneaking behind Lenehan, eying up the girl. He saw him move into the* café and sullenly swallow his distaste. *And he saw everything in between. Go on, write about us, describe us if you can.* Between Rutland and Ponterosso, where the domestic sounds mixed with the smell of love Lenehan had a moment of thought. He thought about changing his shape, like a fox might in the middle of the night. He could have become gallant. But that would have taken a lot of work. *Easy Mr Joyce, that was not fair. The city may seem small to you now that you're looking out on a Via, but remember all that walking that has to be done, the miles between the cigarettes.* Lenehan was out of his own hands now. *Oh well, whatever you think. We'll get our own backs, we'll get the backroom boys to refuse to print, after all Corley talks to policemen.*

The page flickered on the shadow of a *casa*.

'What,' the tall man bellowed, looking down at Rosa Maria, 'I would have thought you'd hate them.'

'Why?' Rosa Maria asked, looking up at him with one eyebrow higher than the other. Her hair was black, her face illumined with enjoyment.

'Well …' There was a trap here somewhere but he couldn't find it.

'Ah, but I like the way they were imagined. I could hate them but I don't,' she said, her eyes crinkling at the corners, letting him off, saving his fall.

'I see,' Toby said, from the left hand side of the circle, not seeing at all. A woman pushed a teacart on the outskirts and started collecting cups.

The two *boyos* were making good headway to take their places in Sackville Street amongst the crowd, the crowd that moved this way and that, making space for them as if they were joining a Sunday evening choir. Those two streets they'd just graced could be named for heroes.

Papers Number 1, 2 and 3 were about to start, so Ruth rushed away from her coffee and made her way to Room 1904, followed closely by Toby Doyle, who had not until that moment known which choice he was going to make. The man who took to the podium was, surprisingly, every bit as good looking as the picture on the programme, in fact, maybe even better. His hair fell down in tresses around his eyes and he coughed slightly when everyone was seated. He brushed the table with his hand, then looked out straight at the audience.

'Patrick Kavanagh was right,' he said, in a surprisingly deep voice. Ruth would have expected polished slimness in it.

'He was right about Who killed James Joyce/I, said the commentator,/I killed James Joyce/For my graduation.

And he was right about What weapon was used/To slay mighty Ulysses?/ The weapon that was used/Was a Harvard thesis.

But particularly he was right about Who carried the coffin out?/ Six Dublin codgers/Led into Langham Place/By W. R. Rodgers.'

A laugh went up and people settled themselves nicely, they'd be able to tuck into this paper. It would certainly make a change from the last one which was given by a scholar who had translated *Finnegans Wake* into Catalan. 'As if you could know,' said the introducer, causing a deep frown to move over the face of the speaker. And it had never lifted. Then how could it, thought Ruth sympathetically, if you'd done all that work and a slip of a starter could get up and throw that line out of a hangover, you too would keep a frown on your face and heart. But it looked like this curly-headed chap would entertain them.

'I do not intend to become the unwritten verse in Kavanagh's poem. I do not. You are wondering how I will achieve that, well this is how …'

And he lifted his single sheet of paper, walked off the podium and out the door. The participants watched him go, laughed again and waited for him to return. The realisation that he was not going to come back dawned on some people sooner than others. A choice now had to be made, whether to laugh or get indignant.

'Well that's one way of getting out of it if you've nothing prepared,' Ruth said, breaking the silence. TD wished he'd thought of that. She got up to leave and others shifted to follow her. Some made to call in late to other sessions, deciding along the way whether to mention their smartarse, or whether to annoy him by not referring to it at all. Ruth made for the door, deciding to get some unexpected fresh air.

Lenehan slipped out on to the road to look up at the blue Trinity clock. It was always reliable. He thought the 'always' superfluous, but there you go.

Corley said I always let her wait a bit, sweating that this might be just the time she would decide to move forward, decide that the petting of his ego and the mediocre kissing was just not worth the humiliation of having to stand on a street corner, pretending to be excited by the thoughts of him. Funny that men dressed like him were never good at kissing. Him and his oily head.

As Ruth walked around the fence, she saw Stephen in the distance. She'd slept with him once. You could do that now without fear, if so minded, thanks to Carl Djerassi, Luis E. Miranontes, and George Rosenkranz. Of course you could also say that it was thanks to Gregory Pincus, Min Chueh Chang, and most of all to John Rock. No one here might know their names, silly them. The women these men knew must have helped them, tried out their ideas even, made sure that Ruth now had the means not to get caught. She remembered Stephen as a startled lover, a man you could want as a friend.

The touch of the rails on her fingers made her hands hot with history.

There was no cockiness about her but there was something, a hidden pride for being here in this place, it was in all the secret pockets of her. Her grandmother had worked as a housemaid, for priests, doctors and the like. Ruth had only just found out things about her life, for who cared what happened to the girl in the basement. Ruth walked up Grafton Street, took a detour as far as the Conservatory of Music in Chatham Row, past the pub where she'd had a drink last night. She walked by a room where a recital was being prepared. A man was in battle with his own capabilities, eyes occasionally closed to shut out any sense that would interfere. A woman sat turning the pages, perfectly in time, she too must have known the notes. A shot of Puccini wafted out through the slice of opened window – a pigeon got carried away with it and flew into the glass, momentarily stunning itself. It lifted its wing and passed it over its blushing eyes in order to forget the mistake it had made, just like a cat would. Ruth smiled. Now who's lucky she thought, because she was prone to optimism. She should go back now. It was time for the next movement into the understanding of why artists do what they do, and how.

The two boyos had passed the almost naked harp. The music had come whispered to them, like something running under water waiting for its moment to emerge.

It was time for papers 4, 5 and 6. Number 6 was Ruth's.

Paper number 4 was being given by TD himself. As the coffee-break conversation prepared to fall into an echo and the woman on the outskirts rattled the cups, the grin on his face had got wider – it covered the entire bottom of his face now, even falling down into his chin. He straightened himself up and took on a priestly stance. He was pleased with himself. You see he had it figured out. It required a lot of work to do a paper on Joyce. You couldn't just talk about yourself and him, and the effect he'd had on you, or at least the effect you thought he ought to have had on you. All that had been done before, hundreds of times, by people with higher opinions of their own thoughts. But he had it nailed. This time he had nailed it. He had paid Lachey to trawl the most obscure papers given in the most obscure places and he had rearranged them to fit into his own experience. Getting Lachey to do this had been easy enough. The conversation had gone something like this:

'I couldn't do that. How much? Good lord. All right.'

TD was an expert at this, he knew just how much of what to pay in order to get the evening swinging his way. It didn't always have to be money, it could be in another currency, a good word dropped here and there, a bad word dropped accidentally. Hadn't he got a quote of his, among the poets, on the entrance to the labour ward – how else except by some words or deeds somewhere? The fact that there were women who wanted to change their maternity hospital after looking at it for a number of long appointments was neither here nor there to him. He smiled some more. Today was going to be good. He knew how to read Joyce, not everyone did. There were some people who thought that you could decipher it in different ways, he didn't agree, he thought you had to be a particular kind of man to understand *Finnegans Wake*. Woman? Ah no, didn't think so. But the funny thing was sometimes, just sometimes … For instance, he'd like to get close to that Ruth, converse with her, debate some things with her, alright copy some of her notes, if the opportunity presented itself. That way he'd get a new view, because surely she wouldn't have the same thoughts as the rest of the panels. She didn't look as if she would, something about her. She would surely have a fresh and pearly thing to say. Now there was a thought, if he could find Lachey again. Very few people would go to her paper and certainly no one would go to both hers and his, so if he just got the gist of her points he could pass it off easily enough as his own in the summing up paper he had to do for the closing session. Hadn't he managed similar before without notice? Once he'd had a bit of a scare. Some mad woman claimed that he'd taken her essay on the shades of *Yonnondio* in *The Grapes of Wrath* and used the entire premise of it. He laughed it off of course, snorting; who on earth could think that he'd have even heard of the publication, whatever the name of it was. Everyone believed him of course. (He'd found the obscure review in the sitting room of a woman he'd slept with, he was nearly sure.)

'I don't like stealing from a girl,' Lachey said.

'If you're worried about being found out, remember that if you stole from a man chances are someone might have heard it before, but a girl, it's unlikely. You'll never be caught,' TD reassured him.

'That's a terrible thing to say,' Lachey replied.

'Oh there's been worse said believe me and will again. Go.' And Lachey remembered favours given and still needed.

TD looked across the delegates who were gathering themselves together again, dropping their thoughts into their own particular expertise. He smiled at Ruth, she half smiled back, a bit disdainfully he thought. Well, wait until she'd find that only six people were going to her paper and over a hundred to his.

However, that is not what happened.

Lenehan let his hand run along the railings of Dukes's Lawn. Look at it, standing there between the Museum and the Library, it could definitely make a good home for a parliament, wouldn't that be something new.

The delegates moved en bloc to hear Ruth's paper. She stood in the same spot as the Catalan translator, and the Kavanagh lover, who hadn't been seen since, and began.

'Good afternoon and thank you for being here. I know that it can be difficult to decide what are the new things we need to know about Joyce. And I may be about to add to those difficulties because I'm here to propose that the slavey in the Baggot Street house was a real person and, while that might not discommode the work of everyone, it may cause some upset, because I'm here to tell you that she was my grandmother. I have recently been given a letter, found by a diligent librarian among the bits and pieces gone yellow at the bottom of a box belonging to several women, hard to say what belonged to what one. Not much fuss about that then. But the librarian noticed the address and names and sent it on to me, for which I am grateful. She was of the opinion that these things matter, particularly when all concerned are dead.'

Ruth turned the page for the audience to see. The writing was slanted to the left, lying back, looking expectantly up to the top of the page.

Dear Eve, I will not tell you everything that happened today because today was no different than any other day, how could it be, but there was one thing last week. I'll get to that later. I did the usual pot walloping in the kitchen, the usual bed making, the usual emptying, dusting, scrubbing. I tried that thing you used to do to rub the pain from my back and knees. But I still like the house, I like walking about it. I pass the mistress with no sadness in my eyes. They assume that because I'm a maid I was born to be a maid. And that I think like a maid. They love knowing that, although they don't know what a maid thinks like. They do not know that a girl proficient in scrubbing and emptying their chamber pots would have an ambition or two worked out, as well as the way to achieve it. I do hope that your new place is as good and not as bad as here. It will only be for a short time now with your marriage coming so soon. I thought of you the other night when I was getting ready for bed. I know that you were worried about me going to meet the Corley boy, such an idea that he had that we wouldn't find out his name. But you know I always told you that I was well able for him and that the journey on the tram to Donnybrook was something to look forward to. It was worth putting up with his swagger for the interest of it. And he was always nice enough. I didn't even mind him asking me to get him a bit of money if I could. I should have minded but I didn't. The first time he was so grateful. But he never mentioned it the next time and he then put the squeeze on me again. I didn't like that. Not one bit. So last Sunday I was to meet him but I went for a walk with the other maid first, the one from your part of the country, and there he was deep in talk with a friend of his. Both of them were engrossed, so I walked behind them for a bit, luckily not telling the other maid that I knew one of them. I wished you had been here so I could have told you the things they said. I could not believe the way he talked about me. It was all I could do not to get sick when I heard the names he called me. His friend seemed to lap it all up, him and his white shoes. What I minded most was that he took the air from me. I could feel him take it from me. Air, like water and light, has its own space and should not be stolen. But I would not beg for mercy, after the words had wounded me, it's not good to beg for mercy, because if you have to do that they won't give it to you. When I'm an old woman I will have learned a lot, as much as I've wanted, but will there be anyone to listen. Maybe I won't care. I hushed the other maid and listened more, maybe I shouldn't have. I raged to myself, I didn't want to let her know it was me they were talking about. But you know you have to get over boys like that so I thought I would get them some day, maybe not yet, but some day. I would bide my time like an owl waiting for the night. And when theirs came I would watch them eating their words as if they were sand, trying to *spit them and I would not help them, maybe pass them a bit of water, but not much. They were blocking my light with gibberish and they would eventually have to pay. I had to run then to get up to the corner so he'd think I was waiting for him …*

Ruth looked up. 'I'm afraid that's as far as I've got with the letter, I'm having to decipher the faded writing, but I will have more done by our next conference.' Rosa Maria was heard gurgling with laughter in the back row. The applause that came had a spring in it, Ruth sat down, and the wing of the dead writer breathed past her again. A few people came up to speak to her, including one of those fellows who had been looking over her shoulder at the first talk this morning. He lost himself amongst the others as he sidled up to the desk. Interesting. Ruth saw him leave with the paper in his hand. She smiled. He went straight to TD, who wasn't looking very happy.

'You owe me,' Lachey muttered, as he passed over the paper. TD glanced at it. That would do. Do lovely, no one would ever know.

The final session began with a ring of heartiness about it. The participants wound up the learning, some with joy, some with the gusto of truth, and all dedicated to the teaching of literature as a way to understand science, commerce, politics, war and love. TD stood to do the wind up, opened his own notes, did the necessary thanks and then with a flourish picked the last page with confident fingers and a knowing smile. He said, 'It is of course my privilege to have the last word here and I'm delighted to do so,' and then he consulted the page in his hand. 'Today I went into a haze of confusion with my friend, a kind of quick fog fell over us, kept us hidden from the rest of you as we had our brief skirmish with morality.' What the fuck was this, TD moaned, but he couldn't seem to stop himself – 'You will of course know what happened next. I'm a dab hand at getting the deal but putting distance between me and the ooze of corruption, so I came out of the fog looking as clean as a whistle. In the gullet of the street no one would have known what I am really like.' TD frowned, the silence from the room got louder, sweat went down the small of his back. He was at the last sentence. It read, 'You do know that stealing words is the same as stealing money, only worse. Remember this is not over yet.' He swallowed hard, people looked at each other, Lachey grinned widely. Who could tell whether he knew what was on the stolen page or not? People began to snigger, Toby pulled himself together. 'Of course all of this is metaphor.' He turned, gulped the glass of water and left the podium. A puzzled unrhythmic applause happened.

All the walking and the sadness and the seediness brought Lenehan back to the Rutland Square Refreshment Bar, where he had a plate of peas with pepper and vinegar and a ginger beer. Here's where he almost had a change of heart. Here's where the falling silence of those around him made him just a bit uneasy, but who were they to think of him like that. No, he would be fine. He would begin his walk again. He would catch up with them and see how things had turned out.

Ruth stood up and flung her light silk scarf around her neck. She would go to the pub with Rosa Maria and others. She would sip the light of today, while in the far corner of a different place Toby would try to drink some darkness from the night.

Two men walked down the street, they had money between them. They faded into signifi-cance as if they were stepping on to the page of a book.

The Boarding House

Oona Frawley

Mrs Mooney was a butcher's daughter.

No one any longer called her Mrs Mooney; she was only 'Marie', and half of them *looked* at her when she corrected them – 'Marie, dear: like *marry* in haste, repent at leisure'. Sure wasn't that half the problem with the world? Along with the priests, manners had fallen into the ditch. She didn't mind the loss of the priests, now, but the manners – well. And your man above, wasn't he a problem of manners, anyway? Just like the old fella who'd bet her down and up the stairs like a football many times before she went back to her mammy's and said lookit and the two brothers came round. They'd told him what was what and he'd hightailed it, so he had, the bruises snotgreen even from her place behind the curtained window. She knew, yes, she knew how unusual she was – one of many to be smacked round the place and one of precious few in that day who had brothers enough and decent enough to stand the bastard down: they'd had practice already with the da anyhow. She'd never let him see the girls after that, never, because she knew – Mrs Mooney knew – that he would let that seething thing in him at them, and they were children. She'd had the strap across her own legs and back enough as a youngster to want them free of it. So.

And now this one – this one with his fine job and his pressed shirts and his dinners out and the fancy wedding cost fifty thou if it cost a penny. The house with the sunroom and the kitchen island and the solar panels. In Ireland, for chrissake, solar panels! It was like something off Father Ted. Annyway. All that, but then – them solar panels weren't the last straw, either, but a whole load of everything followed. The apartment had been in Bulgaria! She and the ladies who did the aqua-aerobics the few mornings had actually stopped and held on to the pool's coiled rim and laughed so hard that their tummy muscles ached far more than they ever did from the lepping about with the foam noodles.

She knew how to use the iPad – sure hadn't he and Therese bought it for her for Christmas, only the few months before it was all taken back? It hadn't been any bother at all to her to go online and skype the grandchildren who were in New Zealand, and to do her emails. She read The Irish Times online now, sure. So he'd made his first mistake there, hadn't he, when he decided to have a little go for himself – thinking that because she kept it in the box in between times she had no idea how to use it properly. The thing was it was only him who didn't know anything about doing things properly. The shock she'd gotten when she'd accidentally opened the history on the browser was unlike anything else had ever happened. It wasn't like the shock of the suede belt and the bit of brass at the end that snapped its teeth into your flesh, though it brought that to mind. It wasn't like labour either, or any physical pain she could think of. This was like something on Joe Duffy. It was just pure and utter shock. Dear God, it still made her palms sweat to think of it.

She was no prude. Mrs Mooney had realised herself after she'd run her wastral of a husband. There had been occasional gentleman friends with whom she spent time over the years, and she had overcome the whole sex-only-in-marriage thing. Otherwise there would have been places in her body that would retain something of her ex-husband by virtue of his having been the last one there, so to speak. But this – this lacked manners. It baffled her utterly. It looked painful and – unnatural, yes; there was nothing at all natural about the people (because sweet Jerusalem there were never only two) and what they were doing. And the fact that they had no hair where God intended was ab-so-lutely frightening: bald as doorknobs, children, like. She couldn't bring herself to tell the ladies at the pool. Not in the pool, certainly, but not even afterwards when they sat with blow-dried bobs having lattes and a chat. How did you bring that up?

She couldn't say it to the ladies, but she – Mrs Mooney who had run that bleeding husband of hers thirty-two years ago, when she was a lass only with two toddling girls – Mrs Mooney could say it to him. Oh yes and no trouble. She had promised Therese to say nothing, and she wouldn't say much, but he had to be told that this was certainly not acceptable behavior in her house. He was upstairs now, she knew – she could hear him – and he stumbling around upstairs in her house doing god knows while she sat here with The Irish Times he'd brought home from the doctor's office, the eejit, not knowing she'd read it online first thing this morning. 'Twas free, he'd said, since it was closing time. Thinking that was funny, the lousy bastard, and he at his wife's scan.

She had had the first part of the chat with Therese earlier. Mrs Mooney had been gentle with her – Therese was, understandably, a bit delicate at the moment, as big as the biggest (definitely eating too much and thinking that she was entitled to in that mad way the women did now), and not at the end yet, with no house of her own any longer and back in her mammy's with her feck of a husband and the dote of a son. How are you feeling, Therese, and how are things with himself? she'd begun, easily enough. Are ye intimate? she'd inquired. It had been awkward, but she'd pushed on; she had enough powder on her that no blush was going to make its way through. Therese had admitted that things had been difficult, and that the 'intimacy' had been limited, she thought partly by circumstance. It was true things hadn't been great even before they'd moved in, but then there had been a bit of an effort – and, well, now she was pregnant and so tired – and also your man – Therese had said – felt like he was in a *boarding house* now, and that would naturally limit the time they had together alone.

Naturally, Mrs Mooney had added. After promising a last time she wouldn't breathe a word more about it, especially to Ger himself, she had sent her daughter, weeping now with the weight of the whole thing, up to have a bath and a lie down, telling her to pour in the Radox, and had kept the youngster with her, fed him a dinner of thinly-sliced ham translucent and gloriously pink – the best from Terry's butcher's – and cherry tomatoes that the child popped into his lovely mouth like sweets, and rice that she buttered and salted lightly (though she knew Therese wouldn't have approved the salt). She watched him without eating herself, sipping instead at tea in a cup that she replaced on the saucer instead of hugging it like all the young ones. Such a beautiful child: he was dinner all on his own for her, just looking. It was dreadful, though, to think of him growing up and doing and being and thinking all those dreadful things men did.

He was in bed now, and your man would be down soon. Mrs Mooney put the paper aside, neatly folded despite its multiple handlings in the doctor's surgery, and got the iPad out of the box, turned it on, stood it up, and waited for his step in the hall. When after a few moments she heard him, she rose – knowing he would head straight for the kitchen and the ham (*boarding house*, he'd called it) – and, putting her head into the hallway, said, quietly so that Therese wouldn't hear, Can I have a word?

The sun still had heat in it, and Ger lingered in the child's room after he put him down, looking at the coloured sky through the curtains, listening to his boy's breath behind him. The rooftops were a mess of shapes against that volume of colour, chimneys and aerials and satellite dishes, electricity poles and the slopes of wire such a contrast to the straight simplicity of the sky which was only itself, tangerine and lemon and fire and blue at once and somehow making sense. To cleave away all of that clutter and stand in the summer evening grass below the sky alone: that would be something.

It was why he regretted the loss of the house above everything. Now they were stuck back in uniform suburbia with its tangles of cables and narrow parking spaces, when what they'd once had was the summer grass and the full sky. He wasn't sure he'd be able to get it back: not that one in particular – with the gorgeous walls of stone plucked from knobbly, sullen green fields, the view of green fields replied to by the blue of distant sea that he had coveted since childhood – but any house like it. All of the years of hard graft gone in what seemed like an instant.

He hadn't been rash. He knew that Marie thought he had, thought that the investment in Bulgaria in particular had been hilarious, but hadn't she been first to yap away to her friends about it? He'd put a bit of stuff by and had been persuaded to go in on it with a few pals. The vision of it had been fantastic. A place they could go in the summer with their families, on a lake, and perhaps visit in winter too, show the kids what real winter was like: Christmas in Bulgaria. Heaps of snow. The kids would learn to ski and they'd have a fireplace as tall as he was; they'd visit Christmas markets and eat warm honey pastries from gloved hands. It would save them money on holidays. Of course now there were no holidays at all, unless you counted the overnight to his parents' house for his brother's fortieth.

He turned to look at the boy, obliviously sleeping there in the wee bed, his brown fringe feathered across his forehead, a bit of milk dried in white cracks where his lips were parted and his breath came in gentle steady sweetness. Watching the lad and thinking how much he had let him down dimmed his vision; he blinked hard to try to prevent his contacts misting. And there wasn't long in it now until there would be another one, and a girl this time. Poor Therese, about to become open and raw again, and they were in this mess.

He was in this mess. That was the truth of it. And Marie was downstairs, looking forward to the fact that he would have to face her – he knew this because Theresa had been crying and crying, uncontrollably in that scary way women had when they were hugely pregnant, asking him what they were going to do. How could she live with him now, she'd asked. Why had he done it? What in the world was he thinking? Did she not satisfy him? She had been choking at that stage, purpled rage and frustration on her face, yes, but also the embarrassment of it – having to ask him, having to have a discussion about their sex lives in her mother's house, at tea time, with their small son waiting to go to bed (he had been in the bath, there, splashing about in the en suite, so the conversation was hissed).

He didn't know. He wasn't sure why. He'd had nothing to say, nothing at all, except to apologise over and over again and say he hadn't meant it. Hadn't meant what? she demanded. How could he explain? And where to start? Did you go back to the hard-won stash of the few Playboys when he was a teenager? That hardly seemed fair: sure all of Ireland had seen those. This isn't normal, Therese had spat at him, her fury dementing her voice to something low and uneven and scarred. He mulled this over more than anything else she had said: he'd never thought of it that way.

When Therese had kicked him out of the room, he'd rung his brother Cian, the older by just eighteen months – Irish twins they'd always been called – and after a bit of what's the craic he'd broached it. Listen, he'd said, perched on the edge of the bathtub with his back to the lad with his ducks. How much d'ya look at the old porn? Hardly ever, Cian said, laughing. Are you taking some kind of a survey ya pervo? Hardly ever? It had astonished him. He'd asked what hardly ever meant and had been shocked. Once a month, once every few months – jaysus he couldn't think of a day without it, never mind a month. He'd told him, of course, why he was asking, and Cian had split his sides laughing at him. He'd laughed too then and after Cian had told him not to be a git and to keep apologising like fuck to Therese, he'd agreed and gotten off with the usual bye-bye, bye bye bye bye.

But it hung with him, the knowing that his brother – his brother, like – hardly looked at the stuff anymore. Maybe it wasn't normal.

He'd go down now, now that the sun had lost its fight and the air was thick with evening. Get it over with and walk into the room, watch a bit of telly while Marie silently seethed at him and his ways, when what he wanted to do was crawl into his own bed with his wife's warmth in it and huddle into a ball, hoping that she would hold him and tell him that it would be alright in the end. He didn't dare go to the door, though. What got at him was the weight of his phone in his pocket, and the need to take it out, power it up and – there. Itch that itch, back to the child, heart against the wall, tears rising.

Therese lay for a long time on her side of the bed, crying. She kept feeling like she would stop and then couldn't, didn't; the tears kept streaming down her face, meeting in uneven ribbons under her chin, on her neck. She cried so long that her round belly went into one of the annoying spasms, the rock-hard tension of it such a surprise each time – the madness of this soft skin, soft tissue suddenly suspending its state and clenching. She sat up, holding her belly and ceasing the crying because it frightened her that perhaps she was in turn scaring the life out of the little girl trying to do somersaults in the reducing space. And so Therese sat with a leg half-folded under her and the other with its bare toes resting on the carpet, holding on to the child and breathing and breathing until it eased.

She caught a glimpse of herself in the slice of mirror on the bathroom door, ajar, and sat up straighter, gazing at the proud belly, smoothing the fabric of her shirt over it. She smiled, feeling a bit muddled, slightly distracted and confused. For a moment she thought, sure what does it matter if he's looking at it all the time? But then the fury returned – she even saw the blood return to her slightly swollen face (Jesus she couldn't wait to be not pregnant and have her shapes back). It *did* matter. The cheek of him, looking at it downstairs while she was sleeping above with their baby growing within! In her mother's house. Her belly tensed again and she swallowed the tears, looked up, but then couldn't get the image of a mirror-covered ceiling out of her mind. This was one of the many things her mother had listed off to her in the worsening litany of what she'd seen: the mirrors was the least of it, Therese, she'd said frankly. Who wants to have that conversation with their mother?

He was in with the boy; she could still hear the soft singing, the repetition of *twinkle twinkle* over and over again, the low notes of it in the quiet. Could he hear that she had stopped crying? Would he come in to apologise again after the boy fell asleep? She had told him he wasn't welcome to come back that night, that he should go to his brother's or anywhere, though she knew there was no money for a hotel and that his brother's was too far away when she was this close to term. She'd wanted to mean it, wanted him to hurt and hurt the way that she was hurting now. But the truth was she wondered if she'd be so angry – *you must be devastated*, her mother had said – if they'd been in their own house where she wouldn't have to merely mime her rage rather than release it. Was it being here? Was this what provoked the fury? The terrible displacement, the shame of being past thirty, in the sensible decade, and losing your home?

They'd never even gone to Bulgaria. The tears slid down her face again, but she didn't sob this time. It seemed daft now. She'd give anything to have back the money from the wedding; thinking about the cost rattled her. With that they could even buy a house in Laois or somewhere else in the middle of the country now, a wreck of a place, surely, but a place of their own. They could be in a stone cottage with a massive fire and a wild garden half-full of vivid green reeds and buttercups and coiled fiddleheads, the intricacies of cobwebs visible on those heavy, misty days when the moisture caught like jewels on the threads. The children could roam free and go to a tiny parish school packed with farmers; she would invite the mums round for tea and learn how to grow her own vegetables, and Ger could re-do the house over time, turn the old out-buildings into a workshop or a playroom for the children as they got older. They'd go for walks along famine roads together and never mind about Dublin or expensive restaurants and sun holidays: perhaps they could be happy together.

She looked at her own face directly in the mirror. Perhaps it wasn't too late. She was only thirty-four. They could even go to New Zealand where Bernie was and Ger would be sorted with work. It would be warm and there would be cousins for the children and she could return to teaching when her own were in school. Learn to ski as Bernie had, take holidays in January at the beach. There were lines around her eyes, and the skin was puffed and uneven. He'd ruined it. All of those plans. All he'd had to do was wait, for God's sake. How could she possibly get up to anything in the state she was in? How could she get up to anything here, in this house, where she had to revert to the faintly Madonna-like chastity of her teenage years? When they sat downstairs each evening with her mother watching the nine o'clock news and commenting on the coming weather: oh dear, more rain, her mother would remark. She and Ger shook their heads, or agreed that it was a shame. Ah sure, one would say. Better than a desert, the other would chime in. They would laugh over these lines in bed afterwards and fall asleep smiling.

Her belly tensed again and Therese breathed shallowly and listened. There was no more singing. Was that his step on the stairs? It was – he was going down. The bastard: he hadn't even realised that he should have called in to her again, to apologise, to make sure she was alright. Men were so bleeding thick sometimes. Well, anyway, he wouldn't stay down long. That much was certain. He wouldn't be able to bear her mother's silent treatment, though there was always the chance that she'd repeal her promise and give him an earful. The thought tempted her to go downstairs right away but then she stopped and told herself not to be feeling sorry for him. Why should she protect him and ease his way? Therese picked up her phone and gazed at it idly for a few moments, swiping the screen with her thumb, trying to think of something she could read, or someone she could text. But she didn't feel like it. So she stayed there perched on the bed looking at Facebook, the pictures of her friends and their lives a reminder of something – her own life, maybe, and what was lost. There they were in their gardens in the sun, or on the beach, kids' faces with ice-cream on them, enjoying the only summer they'd had in recent memory. Maybe they would be happy again. Maybe next summer that would be them: in a garden with children and ice-cream cones. Maybe it would all come good.

She flipped through a few recent pictures to see if there was one worth putting up herself, but her belly tightened and she put the phone down, listening. Their voices: so they were talking anyway. Her mother's up and down, never too loud, always conscious of the boy asleep – she was that kind of grandmother, considerate and knowings. And Ger's voice, low as well. He'd be covering tracks and making small talk. What was the point, she wondered, in thinking of it at all? When she should be focusing on the baby. But it was hard, not to think ahead and worry about it. Why had he not waited for her?

She sat, breathing deeply through the tension of her belly as hard as a rock now, when then – yes – there it went. She set herself, pushing and pushing away the pictures of him glued to a screen watching until her mind was full only of the clear as crystal sense of what she had been awaiting the past eight and a half months. And she heard her own voice spiraling in the house as she sprang up, calling for him, the waters everywhere.

A Little Cloud

John Kelly

Eight years before he had seen his friend off at the North Wall and wished him godspeed.

T he phonecall, when it came, was something of a thunderbolt, both to Inky Chandler and to his colleagues in Montrose. It was a woman's voice: English, efficient and posh. Mr Gallaher, she announced, was stopping over in Dublin and was hoping to make contact with a Mr Chandler. Mr Gallaher, she explained, had lost all his numbers but assumed Mr Chandler was probably still working in the same place. Indeed I am, said Inky Chandler, still here. For my sins. Splendid, she replied, and arrangements were quickly made for later that evening: The Merrion Hotel at 7pm sharp. Mr Gallaher, she said, was very much looking forward to seeing him again.

Inky Chandler, quite breathless from the call, surveyed the office, open-plan and desolate. His colleagues were surely wondering what was going on. Perhaps they thought the lady on the line was *his* agent rather than Gallaher's and the thought pleased him so much that he began to giggle, slightly, to himself. And for the rest of the day, as mobiles chirped and photocopiers chundered, a rather giddy Inky Chandler looked forward with swelling excitement to the moment when he would see his friend once more. Soon he would be sharing the very secrets of a writer's life and hearing all the darkest literary gossip from New York – a great metropolis in which Ignatius Gallaher was now fêted as an Irish writer of import, perception and wit.

Inky Chandler was called Inky because he was, in all things, miniscule. He was Inky-Dinky Chandler, a delicate little bird of a man with a child's hands and a row of baby teeth which sat like little half-sucked mints behind his nervous lips. His face was smooth and moisturised, and beneath his mousey hair – cropped and tipped with gel – the raw and even violent redness of his skull seemed at odds with his quiet, creeping manner. But as he sat at his desk in Montrose, newly scrutinised by his curious colleagues, he felt as if, already, he had increased, just a little, in both stature and significance. And as he looked out the windows at people coming and going in and out of the car-park with their briefcases and laptops, all of them talking with urgency on their cell-phones, he began to feel just a little sad. He was prone to a certain melancholy, after all. He understood that struggling against fortune was pointless but even so; these sadnesses, such as they were, were of the gentle and accepting kind and, in ways that he could never quite explain, they were often mildly pleasurable.

As the hours passed, with little work being done in the public service, Inky Chandler thought about the notebooks he tended at home. He had a shirt-box full of them; Moleskine mostly, filled with ideas for poems and sequences of poems; sudden lines and similes and even the odd completed couplet or verse, all written in his very neat hand on every second page. And yet, to his shame, no actual completed work existed. He just never seemed to hit on anything which might survive the actual time required to bring it on. Yes, now and again, he'd get slightly fired up and would maybe even consider showing something to Anne, but then the old reticence would get to him, the hanging-back he had inherited from generations of Chandlers, and he'd think better of it. Then, other times, he'd flick through the pages, read random notes and think, yes, not bad at all. And this would please and even console him – as if a breakthrough was actually possible, and maybe even close. This and more he would discuss with Gallaher later. His old friend was never a poet but he would help him. A few pointers perhaps. That was all he needed after all – a little bit of a push.

By 5:20 Inky Chandler was already standing on the northbound platform of Sydney Parade DART Station. People were lined up on both sides, all of them en route to resuming their small domestic lives in conditions which Inky Chandler knew were, more than likely, intolerable. But he had little time for them even so. Dullards, he thought. Ciphers, the lot of them, with their ready-meals and their sneaky cigarettes, and not the slightest clue, any of them, that they were now standing at the very spot where Mrs Emily Sinico had died at the age of forty-three, hit by the ten o'clock slow train from Kingstown. These people were robots. They were ants. No poetry in their lives. No art. No heart and no soul. And as the DART sucked Inky Chandler into Dublin City, in through the dripping gardens of Sandymount and Ballsbridge, tennis-courts and glass-topped walls, past illuminated hockey pitches and the silvery Aviva and finally into the green light of Pearse Station, he took no interest in any of it. Not today. All he could think about was the moment in hand, and the fact that his old friend Ignatius Gallaher would be waiting for him at the bar of the five-star Merrion Hotel. Too early, though. He'd have to stroll around for a bit. Kill some time. Compose himself.

Inky Chandler had never been in The Merrion Hotel before, though he had passed it often enough. The doormen wore grey livery with top hats, and there were always blacked-out limousines pitched outside; paparazzi too, set to ambush movie stars or pop singers. And the walls of the place, were, by all accounts, covered with great art. Jack B. Yeats, Patrick Scott, Louis le Brocquy, Evie Hone. And wasn't the Duke of Wellington born in it? Or maybe beside it? Or behind it? In a stable, wasn't that the story? Anyway, somewhere in the vicinity and there was a plaque on the wall. And then that restaurant Guilbaud's where they served all sorts of fancy dishes. A newsreader at the quare place had once boasted of eating quails eggs and suckling pig, but Inky Chandler thought it all sounded a bit too rich for him. That sort of thing was only for the famous and the well-to-do, men in black tie probably, and stooped women in noisy dresses and high heels they couldn't walk in. But then this evening was all rather different. He was to meet his friend and colleague and he would have every right to enter and remain.

Of course, a place like The Merrion would be no bother to Gallaher. He was always a bit of a swank and was never short of money either. Even when he was still writing for the papers and running all those websites, he'd always be up to some scam or another. If there was funding to be had, from whatever source, he'd be in like a shot. Big money in the culture business, he used to say. All you have to do is learn the language, get the old shtick off-pat and they'll just throw the moolah at you. Some people used to say that he was nothing but a hustler – a charlatan even – and of course he did get into bother over that Government money he got for some project which never happened at all. It was an unfortunate business right enough – in fact, people said it was the real reason he went to America – but you had to admire him, all the same. The neck. You're never dead till you're in your bed, he used to say. Let the dog see the hare. That was another one.

It was still far too early, so Inky Chandler walked right past the front of The Merrion, across the street and up into Ely Place. At the corner of Hume Street a young woman sat on the footpath, her back against a giant silver lamp-post, a blue hospital blanket over her legs and her belongings – what she had of them – secured in a plastic bag between her knees. Inky Chandler observed all as he swerved and skipped past. Skin yellow, hair scraped back, features blunt and mouth hung open like … like a *communicant*. That was a good one. He'd have to remember that. The woman asked for help, for a hostel he thought, but Inky Chandler refused to turn around. The city had gone to Hell, he told himself. In a handbasket. But *communicant*. There was something in that. They would never expect a word like that from Inky Chandler – and him of the other persuasion. They would expect something more biblical perhaps. *Behold, there ariseth a little cloud out of the sea, like a man's hand.* Something along those lines. But *open mouthed like a communicant*, that was a good one. Original too.

It was at moments like these, alert and inspired, that Inky Chandler really wished he could record his thoughts on paper, or on a dicta-phone maybe; men in sleeping bags already settling into doorways, children – actual urchins you might say, and malnourished by the looks of it – coming out to scavenge and to rob. Two drug addicts attempting some sexual act on the wheelchair ramp of Iveagh House. And wait! Had he passed the Office of Public Works yet? He had. Then Newman House and a hen night astray. A night of hens. Belly tops, they called them. Spilling, flabby bellies. Feather boas. Then the Unitarian Church and the Royal College of Surgeons and the LUAS slipping by. The bells of the LUAS. The *campanology* of transport, he thought. Must write that one down too. Harcourt then Charlemont and on to Bride's Glen. All aboard for the sightseeing tour! Then Grafton Street and Fusiliers' Arch and the horses and carriages and fundamentalist preachers: *Prepare thy chariot, and get thee down, that the rain stop thee not.* The taxi rank circulating and then on towards the Shelbourne. A man from work. Ivy on the walls and back to Hume Street and the girl with the blue blanket from Holles Street. Still there. The devout communicant. And then another lap.

Inky Chandler usually preferred the narrower, darker streets; quiet, teasing streets with gentle footsteps and a furtive shuffling that often scared him just a little, but now because he was so near to his rendez-vous, he thought it best to stick to the broad pavements which circled the Green. A few more laps around and it would almost be time. And as he walked in the dimming light he was like a new man with a new step and, for the first time in his life, he began to feel a little superior to the whole thing, both to the city itself and to everyone in it. Dublin was decaying fast and its citizens were banjaxed and lost. There was no doubt about it: if you wanted to do well in life, you simply had to leave. That or be run out of it. But one thing for sure, nothing worth-while could ever be achieved in this sorry place. Not any more.

And as the time approached, Inky Chandler began to sense that he was, finally, getting closer to somewhere else – to Manhattan, say – a place where he might actually live. Flourish was the word for it.

Blossom. Or Bloom. If only he could write down these feelings, these thoughts, these sensations in his actual soul, he would surely find an audience there, and his own delicious melancholy would only stand to him. The critics would welcome him, surely, as a new Irish voice – although he might have to do something about his name. He wouldn't wish to drop Chandler altogether but, just so there'd be no doubt as to his literary line, he could go maybe go for something more Hibernian and double-barrelled like T. Chandler-O'Brien, or T. Reilly-Chandler or R. Chandler-Connolly – although perhaps a surname with the odd *fada* might be better again. He would ask Gallaher about it. Ó Gallachóir. Helper of the Foreigner. He would have a view on it. He would know.

He was so lost in his thoughts that he almost forgot the time and only made it to the steps of The Merrion with two minutes to spare. Out of breath and sweating, he was greatly relieved to see that the doorman was no longer stationed on the stoop. But once adrift inside there was no avoiding a receptionist on the constant *qui vive*. Good evening, sir. Do you need any assistance? No, thank you, I'm grand. Bathroom first. Freshen up. A little mouthwash. Scrub the hands. Grand, thank you, yes and the WC is where? That way, sir. Through there, and the bar is through that door and to your left. Oh, yes. Have a nice evening, sir. Yes, thank you. A minute to seven. Perfect. On schedule. On the button.

The deep calm of the bar held Inky Chandler in the doorway. Looking from table to table, feeling as if he was the one being observed, Inky Chandler tried to cut a serious pose: a slight frown, a purse of the lips, as if he were intent on some very important business. But no heads turned in his direction and when he scanned the room once more he realised that Gallaher had not yet arrived. He stepped in tight against the end of the bar, right beside the cash register and, stepping aside three times to allow a waiter to carry off a tray, he twice declined to order a drink, adding that he was waiting for someone – a resident of the hotel. Perhaps you'd like a seat, sir? No, I'm grand, thank you. Quite comfortable here. Just waiting for someone. A few minutes later Gallaher appeared at the door.

'Inky Chandler, you little bollicks! How are you?'

'Ignatius! Hello!'

'Sorry I'm late, man. Had to take a call.'

Ignatius Gallaher checked his phone.

'19:06. I didn't keep you too long, did I?'

'You're grand, Ignatius. Only just got here myself.'

'Good stuff. Right, so what are you having? Whiskey for me. Two? On the rocks, Inky? Splash of soda? Drop of water? Two whiskies, young man. Straight up. And so how the Hell are you, Inky? You're looking well. How long has it been? Fucksake but we're getting old. Do you think I've aged much, Inky? A bit grey at the sides, eh? And thinning a bit on the roof?'

Gallaher bowed and pointed so that Inky Chandler might examine the top of this head. Inky said he was looking very well and not to be talking nonsense, but Gallaher was indeed extremely thin on top; several ragged wisps which seemed a rather hopeless garnish to a face which had grown long, lumpy and pale. Yes, his eyes were still as blue as ever, but the bright yellow shirt was an unfortunate choice and did little for his complexion. The grey stubble didn't help either. For effect possibly, but whatever the intention, it struck Inky Chandler that his friend had somehow developed the look of a man slightly poisoned by some unyielding element.

'I'll tell you one thing, Inky. The book-writing is hard going. They have me running from pillar to post. Deadlines. Press tours. Readings. Signings. Jesus, it would wreck your head if you let it. Now, I'm not complaining but it's no bowl of cherries, I can tell you. Anyway, I'm glad to be home for a couple of days. Do you want a drop of water in that?'

Inky Chandler encouraged a very long pour.

'Jesus, you'll ruin it, Inky. You know what they say about water and fish. I always drink mine neat. Unpolluted.'

'Ah, I don't drink so much these days. Unless I run into the old crowd or something.'

'Sure you were never a drinker, Inky. Never had the constitution for it had you? Anyway, here's to us. Old times and all that.'

Glasses clinked. The toast was made.

'Come to think of it,' said Gallaher, 'you know who I met today? Bartlett. Looked in a bad way. What's the story there?'

'Not good.'

'And what about Ryan? Last I heard he had some cushy number in Foreign Affairs.'

'I think he's in Brussels or somewhere.'

'Met him one night in London. Like a pig in shite. Sorry to hear about Bartlett, though. The sauce?'

'No surprise there, really. And that's not all he's at either.'

Ignatius Gallaher laughed. 'Jesus, man, you haven't changed a bit. The same oul' biddy that used to give out to me when I'd be on the lash. Tell me, did you ever get off your arse in the end?'

'What do you mean?'

'Well, did you ever go anyplace?'

'I did of course. London. Edinburgh with work. Oh yes, a few places.'

'Fucksake, Inky. Get yourself off to Amsterdam or somewhere. Or Vegas.'

'I hear that place is tacky beyond words. Have you been?'

'Sure have.'

'And is it as vulgar as they say?'

'It's fucking brilliant, Inky. Not for everyone, I grant you, but I'll tell you this much, you can get anything you want in a place like Vegas. Know what I mean? What's your pleasure, treasure?'

Inky Chandler finished his whiskey and, after several attempts, managed to order another.

'I've seen things out there, Inky, that would take the eye out of your head. Just get yourself comped a nice suite with a big circular bed and the almighty dollar will take care of the rest. You should try it yourself sometime, Inky. But then again, maybe it wouldn't be the best idea for an upstanding fella like you. Wouldn't want you getting a heart attack or something. And you compromised, if you get my drift.'

Inky Chandler's whiskey arrived and Gallaher uttered the previous toast once more. Inky Chandler said nothing, silenced by his friend's dark hints of adventurous sex on circular beds and, by the sounds of it, all of it bought and paid for. But then did he actually mean, or even realise, what he was saying? Surely it was just some kind of sleazy bluff? Or was he actually boasting about it?

'I sometimes get the impression that there are no standards over there at all. That anything goes.'

'Well, they sure do believe in enjoying themselves. And sure aren't they quite right? And they love the Irish too. I tell you, man, as soon as I open my mouth they're ready to ate me up. Seriously, Inky, you don't know what you're missing. Vegas is one wild spot ... and New Orleans is another one. It can get pretty crazy there too.'

'It's a wonder you can find the time to write.'

Ignatius Gallaher wiped his mouth with the back of his hand and eyed his old friend.

'For fuck's sake, Inky, you're making an awful production of that whiskey. Get it down you, man. And let's get two more in.'

Inky Chandler took several hurried sips and a very deep breath. Ignatius Gallaher pulled a long cigar from his pocket and angled it under his nose.

'I hate the way you can't smoke anymore,' he said. 'Would you like one of these for later, Inky? Although I should say that these are very good cigars, and I wouldn't want to waste one if you're only going to take two puffs and keel over.'

'No thanks, Ignatius. I don't touch them at all.'

'Did you ever partake, Inky?'

'Not really.'

'I don't suppose you'd like a little bump would you?'

'A little what?'

Ignatius Gallaher chuckled.

'Look, Inky, I'll tell you what I think about places like Vegas and I'll tell you about morality too. There are two worlds out there, Inky. They run in parallel, you might say, and most people live in the one where you suffer and fret and fear the worst. Meanwhile, in the other one, people are having a fucking ball. The rule book has been thrown away,

Inky, and you can do exactly as you damn well please. In *that* world, you can have whatever it is you want. As long as you forget about the stupid rules, that is. Life's a feast, Inky, and you should eat every last thing that's put in front of you.'

Ignatius Gallaher took a long, deep drink, rolled the glass across his forehead and then began, with the slow precision of a connoisseur, to summarise the sexual specialities of several of the world's greatest cities. In many cases he spoke, he said, from personal experience, again talking of a parallel world in which the rich and famous did exactly as they desired. No rules for the liberated, he said. And then he told a story about a well-known movie actress, her husband and a string quartet, which he insisted was true and which made Inky Chandler's throat go very dry.

'And that's how the world works, amigo. And here we are in dear old Dublin where butter wouldn't melt.'

'You must be very bored.' said Inky Chandler. 'Given what you're used to.'

'Well,' said Gallaher, 'this is a bit of a break I guess. A touch of relaxation never did anybody any harm. And after all, sure isn't it home? The auld sod and all that shite. But here, Inky, tell me about yourself. Bartlett told me you got hitched.'

Inky Chandler blushed. 'Sixteen years now.'

'Well good luck with all that. I didn't know your address or I'd have sent flowers or something. Put it there, my man.'

Inky Chandler and Ignatius Gallaher shook hands.

'Any sprogs?'

Inky Chandler blushed once more. 'A daughter. Sorcha. She's fifteen.'

'Ah, that's nice. Just the one is it?'

Inky Chandler looked at the carpet. 'Yes. Just Sorcha. And sure one's enough, eh?'

Ignatius Gallaher punched his friend on the arm. 'Good man, yourself, Inky. I never doubted you!'

Inky Chandler looked at his glass and chewed his lip. 'I was wondering, Ignatius,' he said finally, 'if you might like to come around to the house and meet Anne – my wife that is – and Sorcha, of course. Have a bit of dinner. Maybe we could ...'

'Thanks buddy, but I'm leaving in the morning. I know I probably should have called earlier in the week but I didn't have your number. And the time just flew in.'

'Well, what about tonight then? It's early yet. We could take a taxi. It's not far.'

'Nah, sorry, Inky, can't. You see I'm over here with another fella, a writer from Brooklyn actually, and we're invited to a little gathering later. But sure, you never know, the next time I'm over we could maybe arrange something. I'd invite you along tonight but it wouldn't be your thing, Inky. Definitely *not* your thing, believe me. And you a married man and all.'

'Yes well, the next time you're over.'

'That's a date, so. Scout's Honour.'

Inky Chandler checked his watch. Almost eight o'clock.

'We'll just have another one before you go.'

'It'll have to be quick,' said Gallaher. 'I have to be somewhere in fifteen.'

Inky Chandler ordered two large ones. He wasn't much used to any kind of drink, never mind whiskies on an empty stomach, and his wits, heightened by the alcohol and by Gallaher's refusal, were now beginning to zigzag, pulse and shift.

The simple excitement that had propelled him all day long suddenly evaporated and all that remained was a crimson flush in his face and a sharpened flint of understanding in his soul. This encounter was an ugly business after all; Gallaher was only patronising him with all his bonhomie, just as he was patronising Ireland by coming back in the first place.

'Sure who knows,' said Inky Chandler, pushing Gallaher's glass towards him, 'if you ever do come back, we might be drinking a toast to Mr and Mrs Gallaher?'

Gallaher picked up the glass and held it before him. 'No bloody fear of that. Enjoying myself *far* too much.'

'Ah, you will, someday,' said Inky Chandler.

Gallaher turned to face his friend. 'You got to be kidding, Inky. Married? Me?'

'Well, if you can find the right woman, that is.'

Inky Chandler felt the heat spread across his scalp. He knew he had betrayed himself but he didn't flinch from Gallaher's gaze, the blue eyes scrutinising him with a new uncertainty and care.

'Well if I do,' said Gallaher finally, 'she'll be from that parallel world I was telling you about. She'll be an open-minded one, that's for sure. Remember what I told you about that actress. Well, imagine coming home to that every evening. That's the only kind of wife I'd be interested in. Open minded, free spirited and extremely fucking flexible.'

Inky Chandler shook his head.

'What are you shaking your head for? I'm an Irish writer in New York for fuck's sake. I could have any woman I wanted. Marriage? No fucking way José.'

Gallaher finished his drink and gazed thoughtfully at the bottles behind the bar. And then he made a sudden face, as if he had just coughed up a little sick. 'It must get terrible stale,' he said.

Inky Chandler sat by the reading lamp in the front room. It was a quarter to nine. Not only had he missed his dinner, he had forgotten the milk and the bread – wholegrain or wholemeal, he was never quite sure which. He'd have to go to the garage before Anne got back from her book club. He looked up at her photograph on the mantlepiece; a white-knuckled pose in that blue dress he had bought her in Brown Thomas – for all the thanks he got. And what an ordeal that was! Waiting until the floor was almost empty before finally approaching the girl with the make-up and the mad eyelashes. Have you any idea what size sir? Bigger than me, is she? Smaller than me? What about the bust? About my size? Smaller? Or about the same? And he was mortified. How did men ever go in there and buy underwear – lingerie – for their wives? Or for their girlfriends even? The girl draped the dress across her breasts and Inky Chandler mumbled towards it, so shaken by the whole thing that he forgot his change and had to be called back when he was already halfway down the escalator. And then when Anne saw her gift she was so astonished that she kissed him on the forehead and said it was very trendy. But then when she heard the price she threw it on the sofa and asked did he think they were made of money. She wanted him to take it back first thing in the morning but after trying it on, she thought she looked well in it and she asked him what in God's name had come over him.

Inky Chandler stared hard at the photograph. Not a trace of a smile in his wife's blue eyes. Beautiful eyes but cold. Something mean in them. No feeling, no passion and certainly no love. Not for him anyway. And then he thought of all the women Gallaher had talked about earlier, and he wondered what it would be like to be loved by eyes full of passion – Spanish eyes perhaps, or Japanese eyes, or Scandinavian eyes of lightning green. And why then, he wondered, had he married the eyes in the photograph? The eyes of a woman who didn't even appeal to him in the slightest? And why was he still living with her? Someone who hated him because she hated her life.

His questions startled him and he looked around nervously. And yes, the room was mean too. Mean and prissy and prim and that was all her doing as well. She had bought everything in the very same shop and most of it hadn't even been paid for yet. And as he stared at the coffee table with its wicker legs and its glass top and the stale potpourri, a dark and dull resentment against his own life began to spread deep inside him. Could he never escape from this little house? Might he ever be free of that loveless, hateful woman in the photograph? Could he ever flee to New York? Or even London? And was it really too late for him to live his own life? His actual life, that is. A life like Gallaher's perhaps. If only he could get his poems on paper. Get them published by Faber & Faber. Or Jonathan Cape. That would change everything. And then he could live.

He lifted a ruined volume of Byron from the shelf.

Hushed are the winds and still the evening gloom,
Not e'en a Zephyr wanders through the grove,

A Little Cloud

Whilst I return to view my Margaret's tomb
And scatter flowers on the dust I love.

He stopped. The poem was pulsing in the room. He could feel it. The melancholy of it. And he wondered if he could ever write like that – not exactly like that because writing like Byron would get you nowhere – but if he could just express his own melancholy in some similar way. And there was so much he wanted and *needed* to express. Like the way he felt earlier as he walked around the Green. He could attempt it now if only he could get back in the mood.

But then from upstairs a loud and sudden rumble. It was Sorcha. He had assumed from the lack of thumping music that she was out.

Within this narrow cell reclines her clay,
That clay where once ...

And then another thud from above. Then heavy footsteps. Bangs and slams.

'Sorcha! What are doing up there!'

A loud crash. A clatter. It was useless! He couldn't even read in this house, never mind write. There was always some damned racket somewhere: a smash or a spill, some flare-up between mother and daughter, or mother and father, or father and daughter or, sometimes, all three of them at once.

'Would you be *quiet* up there! Sorcha! Please!'

No response. And as the silence thickened into nothingness, Inky Chandler decided he'd better go up and check that everything was alright. In the bathroom, at the top of the stairs, he found Sorcha on her knees by the toilet bowl.

'I'm alright,' she said. 'Just leave me alone.'

Inky Chandler remained in the doorway. 'Have you been drinking again?'

Sorcha kept her head in the bowl. 'Just leave me alone, will you.'

'Were you in the park again?'

Inky Chandler knew about the park. He knew what went on in the park. 'Well, this is just great,' he said.

'Where's Mum?'

'Sorcha, you're fifteen years old! You can't be doing this.'

'Piss off!'

Inky Chandler stepped across the bathroom floor and leaned in close beside his daughter's ear.

'Have some respect,' he whispered, 'for yourself.'

'Where's Mum?'

'She's at her book club.'

Sorcha raised her head. Her eyes red, her mouth raw, puke lumped in her hair. 'Yeah right,' she said. 'The book club.'

'And what's that supposed to mean?'

Sorcha sank her face deeper into the bowl.

'Fuck off, Dad,' she said, 'you're such a loser.'

Inky Chandler straightened up slowly. 'And you,' he shouted, 'are nothing but a tramp!'

Sorcha's hands tightened on the rim of the bowl. Inky Chandler balled his little fists and began to tremble. 'And another thing, Sorcha. You didn't lick it off a fucking stone!'

A sharp pain shot through Inky Chandler's brain and his heart thudded behind his ribs. Sorcha didn't move at first but then came the sobs and Inky Chandler went back downstairs. He tried to sit, he tried to read, he tried to think, but all he could hear was the sound of his daughter crying. For a solid half hour she sobbed loudly and desperately and yet there was nothing he could do. He yelled twice at the ceiling but it only made her worse and the cries turned to actual wails. And all he could do was listen, even when she cried so hard that she began to gasp and choke, only to resume the moment she got her breath back. And Inky Chandler remembered when she was a baby, crying uncontrollably from some tiny pain coursing inside her, and how she would lose her breath, sometimes for four or five seconds and he would get so frightened – counting seven or eight sobs without a break between them. There were nights it was so bad that he thought she might even die. What if she dies, Anne? If she dies!

The front door opened.

'What the fuck is going on here? I can hear that the length of the street!'

Hearing her mother come in, Sorcha began to wail even louder. Animal noises.

'Nothing, Anne,' said Inky Chandler. 'She was in the park again and I ...'

'What did you *do* to her?'

Inky Chandler's wife glared at Inky Chandler. She stank of booze and cigarettes and the hatred in her eyes was pure. He held her gaze for a moment and his heart closed tight.

'I didn't do anything,' he said. 'I didn't do anything.'

She hurled her bag at his feet and ran upstairs. 'Sorcha, love, what's wrong?'

Inky Chandler listened to the voices above him: the sobs, the mutters, the comforting hums of babyhood, the intimate mumbles of mother and daughter. Of his own daughter and his own wife. And, at last, when the silence came, he knew they were asleep. Both of them dead to the world on Sorcha's tiny bed. He tilted the lamp from his cheek and, filled with shame, he cried his first ever tears of remorse.

Counterparts

Belinda McKeon

The bell rang furiously and, when Miss Parker went to the tube, a furious voice called out in a piercing North of Ireland accent: 'Send Farrington here!'

Morning climbs towards her over the black ridge of the Brooklyn-Queens Expressway, and already she has been with them for hours, and the hours have passed like minutes, and the milk in her coffee has become an ultrasound: tawny, speckled, indifferent to her gaze. Tweet that, Elizabeth thinks, fingertip poised for the camera icon, but in the next instant she has drawn back her hand: someone she does not know will only tell her something she knows too well.

She is scrolling. She is staring. Awake in the pinched, narrow way that the screen brings on, and late for work, and hungry; the hunger has been at her for a while. But breakfast is beyond her: all of that moving. All of that doing. The fridge and the eggs and the saucepan which will need scrubbing; the hob and the knob and the little blue flame. The boiling; the watching of the boil. She wishes that she was Hasidic. She wishes that she was Hasidic, and that it was a Friday night, or a Saturday morning, or whenever it is that their Sabbath falls, and then she would be excused from the expectation of doing any of these things; then, she would simply not be allowed. No fridge-opening. No egg-fetching. No saucepan. No water. No spark. No anything that could be construed as a moment's work – and no seventeen open Safari tabs, either, admittedly, and no radio stream, but she would find a way around that, Elizabeth suspects. She would root out a signal somewhere.

In her office on Suffolk Street, Susan Nolan is thinking tea. Susan Nolan is going on about how essential it is that she make herself a cup of tea, right now, this minute, hashtag something-or-other, a stream of words shoved together like children in a crèche; Elizabeth cannot be bothered to decipher them. Isabel Carney wants tea too; Isabel Carney is on the other side of the city, so this is humour, presumably, this is a little light banality, and now Susan Nolan will ask about milk and sugar, and Isabel Carney will go on about biscuits. And already it is happening, just like Elizabeth knew it would, and at her kitchen table three thousand miles away, her stomach rumbling, her hair unwashed, her finger to the trackpad as though it is a doorbell, and she is saying *let me in, let me in, let me in*, Elizabeth is watching, Elizabeth is staring, and Elizabeth does not know these women: Elizabeth would not recognise either of these women if she met them in the street.

All mornings are like this now. All days. The click, the flit, the skitter. They are talking, the Dubliners; they are multiplying. They are surging, and they are spooling, and they are never stopping; if Elizabeth stops for a moment, as she has done now – just to check in on Facebook, just, then, Gmail – she returns to find that there are more of them, dozens of them, totted up in thin red numerals, waiting to be unfurled. Eight nineteen says the clock on her screen; twenty minutes past one, the voice on the radio says. Elizabeth was in college with that guy, the presenter of the lunchtime programme; he was always asleep on the couch in the DramSoc lounge, his arms thrown backwards over his face. Now he's telling one politician to let another finish, and now he's audibly sipping his coffee, letting the mic get the intimate little catch and kiss of it, letting the second politician drone on.

Jonathan Fisher is angry about *Breaking Bad* spoilers. Senan Finn is providing them. Chloe Devine is angry about bishops, and Richie

Mulligan is just angry; Richie Mulligan is always angry, even when he is tweeting, as he is doing just now, about children's books. Ron Dwyer, speaking of books, has read a novel, not yet published, so noboby else can have read it yet, but everyone must, and two months from now, he says, everyone here will be talking about it. Which is the red rag – 3, 2, 1 – to Valerie Finlay's bull, and here she is, letting Ron Dwyer know that she has read it; that she read it months ago, actually. And here is Nessa Flanagan, whose five-year-old is being wry and precocious again, and Alice Corrigan, with something about Syria – well, fair enough, but not the images; Elizabeth is not going to be caught out a second time by the images: impossible to wipe that sort of thing from your mind once you've seen it at all.

Email. An email. Which gladdens her heart, for a half-breath – vindicates her, for checking, and for sitting here – but which already, as the breath slides clear, has her wishing she had not looked, because it is Arlene Brannigan, of course it is, writing from Dublin, writing from the Department, wanting to know where the press release is, letting Elizabeth know that she has seen her, that she knows that she has been online for nearly three hours now, talking shite.

Dear Elizabeth, the email begins, and Elizabeth can just see her: the ponytail, the diamond studs, the Dorothy Perkins separates. *Hope all's well in the Big Apple on this Tuesday morning (your time!!) Just wondering how the copy is coming along for the Re:Joyce release? We're all so excited to get the details of the festival out to all and sundry, and as you know – as discussed – the ST Culture pages go to print Thursday first thing – our time!! – and we've promised them first dibs on the details. Can I expect it this afternoon (again, our time)? Can't wait to see what you've come up with from perspective of language and overall event thematics and vision! Very exciting.*

Ger McKay is linking to something in the *Guardian* again. Cara Collins, plugging an article; Barry Shaughnessy, plugging a gig. Ian Geraghty's wife has given birth to a baby girl, 7lb 5 ounces, mother and nipper doing amazing. Nuala Byrne's cat is throwing a tantrum. Fionnuala Madigan's cat did something similar a few years ago. Sarah Nolan and Isabel Carney are onto a contest between Chocolate Digestives and Jammy Dodgers now; Valerie Finlay is joining in. Alison Donnelly moaning about the rain. Nathan Austin — Nathan is in Brooklyn, 8:30 now and the New Yorkers are starting to surface — moaning about the snow. Catherine Reilly, RTing a long view of the Liffey that Elizabeth has already seen a couple of times this morning; taken this morning, their morning, around the time there, then, that it is here, now, and no rain, and no cloud, and no filter. The river. The stretch of it. The sky on it. The day flat out ahead; the promise of it. The water, flashing darkness.

The city she could not wait to leave behind.

Let us now praise ungrateful cows. Let us now praise whingers, and self-pity-peddlers, and those who take opportunity, that golden toy, and split its head over and over against the walls of their railroad apartments. *Fucking Hell*, all the Dubliners said to Elizabeth, when she told all the Dubliners what had happened, when the lottery turned out actually to be a lottery, and when a Get Out Of Jail Free card made its way to her, painted green — painted Green — so that at the airport, the people with splayed eagles on their shirtsleeves would let her through, would let her in. *Oh fabulous, New York, oh FABULOUS*, most of the women said, which was from an ad, wasn't it, but nobody seemed to be making a joke. And anyway, they were right.

Are right.

Showered. Her hair wet, but she will wear her wool cap, and pull up her coat hood, and by the time she gets to Varick Street, it will be dry, or near enough. She puts on the blue silk shirt, which is stained from Friday's lunch, but she will cover it with the black cardigan, and her ankle boots have snow stains — salt stains — but the dishcloth will do for those. She wipes them: on the leather's creases the droplets glisten, and the smell of the dishcloth reaches her, rank and layered; she tosses it back into the sink. As she turns, she sees her laptop, closed in on itself like something trying to hide, and her fingers twitch — *a twitch upon the thread*, the Waugh line hands itself to her, the way these things used to do — but no. She cannot manage it. She will not make the train.

Coat. Keys. Gone. Out into the morning, the sharp-aired, hurtling morning. Running to the subway, so no time to check anything, no hands free anyway, gloves on and not the ones you can get now with the little touchscreen surfaces on the finger and thumb; and on the train, body against body against body, and the unseeing eyes of so, so many neighbours, so, so many companions. *Please Stand Clear of the Closing Doors*, the voice over the tannoy says, and nobody stands anywhere but where they already are.

We are where we are where we are where we are.

Re:Joyce is a collaboration between the New York Fiction House and the Irish Department of Culture, which means that Ireland will provide the money and New York will provide the impression of glamour. 'Sexy Joyce,' as Sullivan Barnes, the Director of Fiction House, put it during Elizabeth's interview for the position; looking, in the next instant, wildly panicked that he had stumbled into some sin of the sexual harassment variety, what with there being two women in the room – Elizabeth, and Arlene Brannigan, who had flown over from Dublin for the 'initials', as the grillings in the cluttered meeting room on Varick Street were called – but getting through the panic the same way he got through most things, by running a hand over his bald head and rubbing his palms together as briskly as though he was using them to start a fire.

'Now,' he'd beamed at Elizabeth, 'you're a recovering Joycean, it would seem from your resumé. That must have been fun.'

'God, there can hardly be any other kind,' Arlene had winced from beside him. 'It's very hard, a lot of Joyce, isn't it, really?'

'Very,' Elizabeth had nodded, like the unemployed immigrant she was. 'Which is why I think it's very exciting, what you're proposing to do with this festival.'

'Opening doors,' Sullivan had said, looking to Arlene for affirmation. 'Breaking down walls.'

'God, yeah,' Arlene had affirmed. 'God, yeah. I have to say, the Minister's very excited about it. He loves New York.'

'*Love* that Minister of yours,' Sullivan had said, nodding gravely. 'Love his energy.'

'Oh, he's a fierce man for energy,' Arlene had said, pursing her lips in thought, and then she glanced at Sullivan, one eyebrow arched. 'You wouldn't want to meet him on the golf course, I'll tell you that much.'

'No indeed,' Sullivan had chuckled, palms blurring once more, and Elizabeth had had to fight a strong impulse to spit with aggressive percussion into her own palm, and to extend it to him. For the look on his face – for the look on Arlene Brannigan's face – it would almost have been worth it. But no. She knew the dance. She knew the way to get things done. She smiled and nodded until they were finished it, this round of chortle-and-massage, and when they had finished she gave them an account of her research on *The Spaces of Ulysses* which made her PhD sound like the opening credits of *Fair City*, and she lied about the kind of work she had done at the Writers' Hub in the years afterwards, and the next morning Sullivan Barnes called her and he gave her the job.

The almost-job. The sort-of-job.

Look, there is no shame in it. Not in this city. In this city, you could be an intern at fifty-five, let alone thirty-five, and nobody would think any less of you; they would think you a go-getter, a striver. What was it Sullivan came back from the NEA lunch the other day saying, what term was it he picked up there? A *puncher*, that was it; they would think you a puncher. The fifty-five year old intern, punching your way back into the game. Punching. And hustling. And scrambling. And scaling. And lying. And levitating. And shifting the time-space continuum, and speaking in tongues.

Just the usual intern stuff, really.

At her desk, she writes it on a post-it note and hides it under her coffee mug in case Sullivan sees it: STAY OFF THE FUCKING INTERNET. She knows this; she knows it has to be done. Arlene's press release is an hour's work, if it is even that, and she has procrastinated on it now for as long as it can be procrastinated upon. *Procrastinated upon*: she googles that, just as one last thing before getting down to it, just to check that this is indeed correct, that it is not, instead, *procrastinated on*. General consensus plumping for *upon*, with a few dissenters. A few splinter groups. Which reminds her, there was a bomb scare last night in Belfast: she does a quick search on that too. Nothing exploded. Still, so worrying, that all of that could still be happening; she pulls up Lorcan Clark's profile, Lorcan with the ridey Nordie accent, just to see if he's saying anything of interest, which he is not, really, but anything will suffice just at this moment, even if it's about the Tyrone GAA team, which most of Lorcan's output seems to be, and then, since she's here, she might as well see what the rest of them have been up to since last she heard from them, and then it is plunge and sink and deafen; then it is stare and scroll and drown. Jesus, how can Sarah Nolan and Isabel Carney still be having that conversation, but having it they are, or some descendant of it: *Woot! Woot!* Isabel Carney has just added to the thread. Apropos of which, 'Woot' is a word Elizabeth has long been meaning to google, but no time for that right now; Ron Dwyer and Richie Mulligan are having a showdown, this time about experimental poetry, and Valerie Finlay is in between the two of them, doing her usual plié on the fence. Which reminds Elizabeth to check in on Sarah-Jane Fogarty, whom she does not follow – whom she would not please to follow – but on whom she always keeps a eye; Sarah-Jane is always good for a bout of righteous indignation, and there she is, outraged little fists all up in poor, dimwitted Charlie McIntyre's curls because of something harmless Charlie has said about that model with the lips like draft-stoppers, and so Elizabeth just has a quick shuft at the photoshoot which brought about the offending comments in the first place, and for Jesus's sake, Charlie is spot-on, the girl is a slattern, and, logging in under her commenter profile on A Pint of Plain, the satirical site where the photos are being shown, Elizabeth says just that, not mincing her words, not bothering with more than that one word, actually, and writing it in all caps, in case anybody misses her point.

'How's it coming?' Sullivan says, showing up behind her the way he does, and he raps his knuckles on her desk and then immediately stipples with his fingertips at the same spot, as though to erase any possible interpretation of hostility or intimidation, as though to say, we're all friends here.

'Great,' Elizabeth says, and it is as fast as the firing of a synapse, her hitting of command-H, and if Sullivan has seen anything – word, website, model, draftstoppers, breasts, the red brick of Grafton Street and the shimmer of goose-pimpled flesh – he does not let on. Sullivan majored in International Politics at Dartmouth. Sullivan, she has discovered, never lets on.

'Great,' he says, and he stipples at her desk once again. Elizabeth looks at his hand; his gaze follows hers, and, just for a moment, his hand becomes a fist, in the next moment pulled back to the safety of his trousers pocket.

'Just tweaking,' Elizabeth says, and she gestures, now, to the Word document open on her screen, the one that has been smothered, all morning, under the weight of the Safari tabs, the one into which she has not, in truth, typed a single new line since Friday evening. That line – that fragment of a line, actually, which is all Elizabeth managed to make of it that evening before abandoning the effort at 7pm – is split off and centered on the page in front of her now, the cursor blinking like a hazard light at its periphery; *Immensely influential intellect*, it says, and a couple of inches further down, the words GERALD WEATHERS BLAH BLAH WHATEVER appear to be waiting to jump it. Elizabeth clears her throat.

'That won't go in the final draft, obviously,' she says.

'What?' Sullivan says, seeming distracted.

'The – nothing,' she says, scrolling up.

'So we're on schedule for Dublin, yes?'

'Right as the mail,' Elizabeth says.

'I like that,' Sullivan says, pointing at her. 'I like that.'

'It's –' Elizabeth begins, but Sullivan is nodding; evidently, she does not need to continue.

'It's good. It's good. I think I'm gonna use that. I think I'm gonna add it to the repertoire.' He winks. 'Right as the mail,' he says, in his imitation Irish accent.

'Oh good,' Elizabeth says, and as he walks away, she clicks, and it bounces back up for her, her fat blue stream.

In Lucan, a child has been abducted. Garda Siochána Red Alert; light-colored van, possibly foreign number plate: it is everywhere. As is Anastasia Cleary's photograph; "Little Anastasia" – as she has by now been baptised by the internet – is six, will turn seven next week, and was, just under an hour ago, snatched from the Green at the centre of her housing estate, where she was playing after school. It seems there are plenty of witnesses to the incident, which gives some hope, but since each of the witnesses seems also to be aged six, and since each of them seems, naturally enough, to have his or her own version of the light-colored van and the dark-haired – in some versions, red-haired – male driver, their testimony is likely to be of limited use, and of limited comfort to Monica (31) and Paddy (33) Cleary, who have two other children and 'have found themselves,' according to Herald.ie, 'in every parent's worst nightmare'. Gardaí are confident of a positive outcome, and roadblocks have been set up around the region, and on Twitter and on Facebook, it is high tide with a storm behind it: again and again they are coming, the alert and the appeal for help. Piling up high, one begetting the next begetting the next, and in the face of it all, Elizabeth feels she can hardly not write something, can hardly not add her voice to the swell, and so she tweets it – Here's hoping #findanastasia – and then deletes it, because it sounds like she is talking about a rugby match, and she tries again – Thinking of you, kiddo #findanastasia – and pretty much instantly she deletes, because that sounds frankly creepy, as though she is talking to the abductor rather than the child, and what comes out next – Please God #findanastasia – has to go straight away, because it might have come from the heart, but it makes her sound like someone making an apple tart and clicking her tongue at Liveline.

And then.

Christ, @lizzyfarrell, come on, spit it out, girl! #findanangle

Richie Mulligan.

Her heart bolts; heat crashes her face. Richie Mulligan has almost ten thousand followers – she checks now, to discover that in fact it is closer to twelve – and he has put her name into the body of the tweet, rather than at the beginning, meaning that everyone who follows him – which seems to be everyone she knows – will see what he has said to her. The only mercy is that, without her own original tweets, Mulligan's remark will make sense to nobody but her – or at least, to nobody who did not also notice her Anastasia tweets appearing and disappearing. How many followers can she and Mulligan have in common? A few hundred maybe: he had been the Children's Laureate, during that last year before she was let go from the Writers' Hub, and there would have been a bit of overlap, and they both would have been already on Twitter by then. So that is, say, three hundred of her acquaintances and associates and professional contacts, watching her being ridiculed by this lank-haired gimp with his –

Sorry, out of order there @lizzyfarrell. Not funny at all. And anyway I hear you: hard to know what best to say. Except: #findanastasia

High moral ground? He must be joking. *Go fuck yourself,* Elizabeth has typed and tweeted in response before she can stop herself. She folds her arms and regards it, sitting there: it looks so neat, so calibrated, so right; right as the mail, right as the mail. And *#findanastasia fucking trolls,* she adds, as a coda, which, she reckons, has quite a ring to it, and she clicks through to check for comments on her comment on A Pint of Plain.

Everything has gone Anastasia-shaped here as well. Usually, the posts on this site exist for the purpose of taking the piss, but when something truly serious happens in the country, the editors will run an item, presenting the facts simply, starkly, without any of the usual wisecrackery. They have presented, in this case, only the child's photograph, and underneath it her name, and underneath her name a line about what has happened to her, and underneath that, a link to the

Garda alert page, and in the comments it is all sincerity, all *Appalling* and *Sweet Jesus* and *Every one of us needs to drop whatever the fuck we're doing and look for this child NOW*. And *Prayers* and *There has to be be CCTV* and *If ever anything put my stupid worries into perspective* and *I cannot imagine* and *Check the scrubland, check the ghost estates* and *Oh my God that poor little angel, this is so so distressing* and +1 and ++1 and *Agreed, I won't be able to do a tap until some good news is found* and +1 *Nightmare Beyond Words. Thoughts with the Parents.*

Elizabeth thinks of something, then, and clicks into Facebook to see if either of the parents is on there; *Monica Cleary Dublin* brings up three options, and one of the photographs is of a woman around Elizabeth's age, so she clicks through to that, and finds that the page is private. Which frustrates her, but at the same time impresses her, and at the same time, it strikes her, makes the whole business of the child being taken by – let's face it – a paedophile even more unfortunate, if that were possible, even more awful: to have the luck to be born into a house where your parents possess the intelligence required to set their pages to Private, and then to be snatched away by a half-bred maniac …

The father is on Twitter, though. His profile comes up through Google when she looks for him. He is only an occasional user, by the looks of it: a few boring things about football, and only 41 followers – probably mostly his actual mates – and nothing from this afternoon or even from this week, which is what Elizabeth was hoping to find, with all the attendant pathos, with all the terrible irony. So unsuspecting. So innocent. But no: only something Elizabeth does not even begin to understand, about Arsenal, and one of those embarrassing attempts at a hashtag that makes him sound like someone's Dad.

Or. Well. Not like that. More like –

'Elizabeth,' Sullivan says from behind her, in the same moment as she notices them, the notifications, 42 of them, it would seem; that number, sitting on the little bell icon at the bottom of the screen like an insect, filling it with color, filling it blue.

'One sec, Sullivan,' she says, as her fingertip finds its position on the trackpad, 'Just need to check this one thing.'

'Elizabeth,' he says, in a tone she has never heard him use before, a tone which is enough to make her turn and look at him, and his face is white, and in his right hand he holds his iPad, and with his left hand he points towards Elizabeth, towards Elizabeth's computer.

'Turn that off,' he says.

'But I −'

'Turn it off. You've done enough.'

'But I haven't even −' She stops herself. *I haven't even started*, is what she so almost said, and she has to stop herself, now, from laughing at the near-miss. 'I just need to put the last touches on this bio,' she says instead.

'Forget the bio, Elizabeth,' Sullivan says abruptly.

Something is the matter; she knows this now. It is not Sullivan calling her into a meeting; it is not Sullivan asking her to do a Starbucks run. It is Sullivan looking, with apparent disgust, at his iPad, which he moves towards her now so violently that, for a moment, she thinks he is going to clobber her with it.

'*Find Anastasia fucking trolls?*' he says, holding it out to her. On his screen is her Twitter page, with the − she now sees − deeply unflattering profile photograph she took of herself in the café on Morgan Avenue last month, and displaying the two tweets to Richie Mulligan and the one from earlier this morning, the one about not wanting to have to bother to boil an egg.

Sullivan thrusts the iPad closer. 'Arlene Brannigan emailed me from Dublin,' he says. 'Arlene Brannigan emailed me in a panic, telling me to look at your page.' He taps the screen.

'I can *see* it,' Elizabeth says.

'A child is abducted and you write an obscene tweet about her?'

'About *her*?' Elizabeth splutters. 'It's not about her!'

'A six-year-old child is probably −' at this Sullivan's voice trails off for a moment; recovering himself, he shakes his head. 'You write *this*? With this organisation named in your profile?'

It's true. Well, she had nothing else to put there. And *Programming Assistant*, Fiction House NY has had its benefits; the number of writers who follow her now, obviously only looking for an invitation, but still. Teju Cole even followed her for a while earlier this year, although quickly seemed to decide he had made a mistake; Elizabeth unfollowed him back, out of revenge.

'And you are not a Programming Assistant, I might mention at this juncture,' Sullivan says. 'Or were not. You were an intern.'

'I what?'

'Pack your things,' Sullivan says, swooping his left palm over his crown. 'I want your desk clear in ten minutes, and I want that press release handed off to Jessica effective immediately.'

'Jessica?' Elizabeth says, incredulously. 'Jessica is the archivist! Jessica can't write the –'

'It's a fucking press release for what's just going to be a fucking drinking session anyway,' Sullivan curls his lip. 'Irish writers, learn your trade!'

Elizabeth catches her breath. 'It's *Irish poets*, actually.'

'I'm sorry?'

'*Irish poets, learn your trade*' Elizabeth says. 'It's Yeats. From 'Under Ben Bulben'.'

He is staring at her. 'What are you talking about? What are you saying to me? Ben who?'

'It's a poem,' Elizabeth says weakly.

'And that's another thing,' Sullivan says, snatching up his iPad. He peers at it. '*Oh to be a Hasid? Oh to be a Hasid*, Elizabeth? I mean, what the fuck? What the fuck?'

'It was a joke,' Elizabeth says. 'I couldn't motivate myself to make my breakfast this morning, and –'

'Apart from the fact that you do not say "a Hasid",' Sullivan says, 'apart from the blatant ignorance and political incorrectness exhibited in that, do you have any idea – do you have any *idea* – of the kind of damage you could have given to some of our key friendships on a corporate and giving level?'

'There's nothing actually *wrong* with being a Hasid. It's not like it's an insult to –'

'Hasidic! Hasidic! You do not fucking say "a Hasid"!'

'Ok.'

'You're fired,' Sullivan says, with a toss of his head. 'I should have known better than to hire someone at your life stage as an intern.'

Elizabeth raises an eyebrow. 'That's discrimination,' she says quietly.

Sullivan scoffs. 'Just try it, you antisemitic pederast.'

As he slams his office door she realises that she is shaking; that she is damp on her palms and under her arms. She goes to her email and is met with a wall of bold text; at least 30 new emails since last time, and she closes her eyes; she cannot bring herself to look at the names. She goes back to Twitter, and opening her notifications is not even necessary; the reactions are all over her feed. In A Pint of Plain, her own profile photograph greets her; she, and a screenshot of her tweet, are now the top story, with the headline *Stay Classy*, and a haul, after just – she checks – seven minutes, of 38 comments and rising.

After she has logged off, she stays staring at the dark screen for a moment as though it might give something, as though it might be something other than a flat pane of glass in which she cannot discern even her own shadow.

But they have found the child; so she learns an hour later, when she gets back to the apartment. They have found the girl. So there is that, at least. There is that.

Clay

Michèle Forbes

The matron had given her leave to go out as soon as the women's tea was over and Maria looked forward to her evening out.

I t was a fat person's thing, but he was only ever aware of doing it after he had done it. Conor glanced quickly around the carriage of the Luas but, despite the fact that it was packed with people, no one appeared to have noticed. A moment later he caught himself doing it again: tugging his T-shirt down so that it covered his protruding belly. It was only a matter of habit, his mother had said to him, and there were plenty of people who had much worse habits than that believe you me.

Conor wiped his brow. It was cold, and he was wearing only a blue windcheater over his T-shirt, and no jumper, but no matter what the weather was like he was always sweating. And he liked the T-shirt even though it was a little on the small side, XXL instead of the XXXL which he normally wore. Nonetheless, the colour black looked well on him, he thought. The T-shirt had been a present from his younger brother Oscar, home on a recent break from his job as a Media Rep in Boston. Even though it was raining, Conor had kept his windcheater open on his walk from Capel Street to Stephen's Green, because the

T-shirt cracked him up: a picture on the front of Heisenberg aka Walter White and the words *I Am the Danger* in metallic blue scrawled across the bottom. Really cracked him up.

Conor turned to look out the tram window, catching the large round pall of his face in its reflection. Yesterday, when he was taking a photograph of a cinema timetable off the net with his phone, he had taken a selfie by mistake. Looking at the photo he had been surprised by how much his features seemed huddled together in the centre of his face; like a cluster of eruptions between two colliding continental plates.

Lozenges of raindrops now stretched and dribbled down the window pane. Outside, the black dampness of the night seemed to have licked the streets clean and spread the lights from the houses sideways in pristine streaks, but inside the carriage the air was steamy and tart: a claggy smell of eggs and wet wool. Beside him, closest to the window, a young woman sat texting on her phone, with her daughter – dressed up for Halloween – standing between her legs. The girl, he guessed, was seven or eight years old. She wore a witch's hat and her face was covered in swirls of black and red face paint. The girl was staring at him and making him feel uncomfortable. He shifted slightly, aware that his left buttock had spread itself generously over the lip of his seat and into the seat of the woman next to him. The Luas droned to a halt and with the drag of it his knee pushed in against the little girl's hip. Still texting, the woman placed one arm around the little girl and drew her away from Conor's leg.

Conor checked his phone. It was seven o'clock. The Luas would arrive in Cherrywood by about quarter past and the walk from the station home would take him another twenty minutes. He'd stop off at the mini supermarket on the way – the one beside the huge empty office complex on that road, whatever name it had, he didn't know – as the mini supermarket there always seemed to be open. He would buy two two-litre bottles of Diet Coke, and maybe a few bags of fun-sized Mars Bars, and pick up something else nice if he had enough change. He would log on as soon as he was home. He was looking forward to his evening in. He had it all planned. The house would be empty, he hoped, as his mother said she'd be out visiting friends.

He had been let go from work ten minutes early because Mr Wyrzykowski, his boss, was meeting a potential client in The Gresham at six-thirty. The people at work liked Conor, they all said they were very fond of him. They said that it was unusual for such a big fella to be so tidy and that he was always dependable to do a good job. Bernie O'Doherty had commented that it was nice to still see a young fella who had manners – she called him a young fella even though he was twenty-six. And Marika from accounts always called him a big softie when he brought her in tea: she had never gotten used to the Irish tea and would ask him to make her a coffee instead, and without any complaint Conor would make her a coffee and apologise. And just that afternoon he had brought her in tea again instead of coffee and Marika had said that it was like a running joke between them at this stage and that he was so nice not to get annoyed at her and that she would miss having the laugh if one day he got it right. And Conor had chuckled and his big frame had wobbled, and he'd tugged at his T-shirt, and wondered if Marika thought she might like to spend a bit more time with him because she always seemed to be laughing when he was around. And he decided that he would always make her tea instead of coffee so that they could have a laugh about it. Marika had an unusual lemon tint to her blond hair and had eyes like pale marbled almonds, which appeared to be looking everywhere at once. Conor had thought that Polish people were very serious, but both Marika and Mr Wyrzykowski always seemed pleased to see him and to enjoy his company.

He had been sent to train as an administrative assistant with Mr Wyrzykowski as part of a new initiative run by the Department of Social Protection. Mr Wyrzykowski ran a refrigeration and catering equipment business from a small office on Capel Street. Conor had no experience in administration and no interest in it and no intention of becoming an administrator. He felt the training was a waste of taxpayers' money and that it would be better for someone else, who actually wanted to be an administrator, to be doing it. But if he refused he would lose his dole, and he knew he couldn't survive without his dole.

What he thought he *would* like to do was to make movies. He had a programme on his PC which showed you how. Over the last few months he had spent his time at home putting together movies of things that he'd filmed on his phone. Random stuff that he'd see during the course of his day or on his journey to work or on his journey home. He'd filmed traffic, road works, rubbish that lay in the street, shop fronts that had been boarded up, the homeless that sheltered in the shop doorways, the narrow stairwell he climbed at work, the boxes of invoices stacked in the tiny storeroom, the back of Marika's head. Since he'd finished college two years ago he had applied for a number of jobs in film, mainly as an assistant film editor or in continuity, but he'd had no luck. Some day he planned to cast actors in a movie that he'd written himself, but not until he could offer them some money. Even though it seemed the thing to do these days, he wouldn't feel comfortable asking people to work for nothing.

A heavily-pregnant woman now stood beside his seat in the carriage. Her hair was tied back in a large silver clasp, her closed umbrella dripping onto her shoes, and she carried a bag of groceries. Conor wondered should he stand and let her sit down, or would that offend her? Or would it be worse if he just kept sitting? He tried to catch her eye to offer her his seat, but her gaze was fixed firmly ahead. He thought of tapping her on the arm, but hesitated – that might not be the politest way of getting her attention. He looked out of the window again. Lines of rain were running straight down the pane, then, as the Luas slowed down, they jilted into thin slopes. At Balally the man sitting opposite him rose from his seat to get off. Conor wondered if he should indicate to the pregnant woman that there was an empty seat when a teenager whipped into it. The teenager was talking loudly to himself. He wore a grey hoodie, dark blue jeans and runners which were spotlessly clean, despite the bad weather. The teenager's face was chiselled, older than its years. Droplets of rain rested like glassy pips on top of his heavily-gelled hair. His eyes were glazed yet wide. He asked Conor what he was carrying in his bag. Conor was a little surprised by the teenager's charged eagerness to talk but answered that they were only some internet magazines he had picked up. The teenager asked him what kind of price would he pay for them now, but before Conor could reply the teenager began talking about his cousin in England and you should've seen the bags of Lexapro he had, 'lady pharmaceuticals' he called them, getting them off the internet he was, then mixing the yokes with awful crap, and selling them for fifty pence a piece over there and he was saying to his cousin that he shouldn't be doin that, people ending up in hospital an all, for fuck's sake, and how he wouldn't be bothered his own bollocks doing that.

More people got off at the next stop and the pregnant woman took a seat on the other side of the carriage. What he got a buzz out of, the teenager continued with an edgy flux to his voice, was walking past all them BMW bastards and holding out his key and scratching the fuckin key all the way down the side of the fuckin car, who's posh now, the teenager was saying and laughing to himself. He then halted midstream and looked at the little girl dressed in the witch's hat still standing between her mother's legs. He said to the little girl how much she looked like a real witch and how she was scaring him and was she going trick or treating and to make sure she got lots of chocolates. Conor wasn't sure whether the teenager was actually making a scary face at the little girl or whether it was just his ordinary everyday face. The little girl stared back at the teenager saying nothing, her mother still texting on her phone. The Luas slowed down into Cherrywood station and Conor stood up from his seat. Hey Buddy, the teenager said, good talkin to you, and he held out his hand to Conor. Conor shook it and smiled. You have a good day Buddy, d'ye hear me, the teenager was saying to Conor, and Conor said that he would and that he hoped the teenager would have a good day too; and Conor thought to himself on reflection, as he got off the tram, how easy it was to talk to a teenager even when he is high on something.

The path from Cherrywood station down to the nearest road was fenced on either side with broad slats of wood, a channel through acres of wasteland. 'Namaland' his mother called it. Tied up with shysters, she said, shaking her head. His mother sometimes talked like an aul one, he thought, even though she was only fifty-three, although that was old enough he supposed. She mainly did it whenever she was tired or whenever she was not interested in what was being said. He supposed it was easier for her than paying attention. Rumours of an IKEA coming, she said, or something else new, well that'd be nice, better than that godforsaken stretch of sodden clay that's there, and it would save them having to use the M50 and that bloody rip-off of a toll.

Conor would listen to his mother but had no opinion on the wasteland or the toll or IKEA one way or another. Checking his phone again, now already twenty-past seven and four Facebook notifications waiting — *Gerry Donovan invites you to like his page*, *Please help find Katie who's gone missing*, *Gerry Donovan commented on your photo*, *Gerry Donovan invites you to like his page* — he thought to skirt along the edge of the wasteland. Some of the wooden slats of the fence on the path from the station had fallen away and on the far side of the wasteland a huge section of the green metal railing had collapsed right by the roundabout. The shortcut might gain him a few extra minutes on the way home. He stepped through the gap and plodded over the wet, mucky, uneven ground. The rain clouds weakened above him and the moon appeared as a pinched white button in the sky. The people who had disembarked with him at Cherrywood overtook him on the footpath as he walked. He realised what little difference the shortcut was making to his journey.

He stood under the glare of the fluorescent lights in the mini-supermarket, music belting from the sound system, the shop empty of customers except himself and no one at the checkout. Up in the corner, above the wines, was the flashing red light of the CCTV camera. Conor lifted two two-litre bottles of Diet Coke and two bags of fun-sized Mars bars and put them into his basket. He stood for a moment to think what else he'd buy: he wanted to buy something really nice. He walked to the biscuit and cake aisle and noted a two-for-one offer on the chocolate Swiss rolls. Now that was something his mother would like as well. He took two and walked over to the checkout. He waited. He could feel himself getting hotter as he stood. He closed his eyes and listened to the music of deadmau5 blaring through the sound system. Beads of sweat rolled down his back. The harshness of the fluorescent lights stung his eyes when he opened them again. Still no one came to serve him. He decided to use the self-service checkout.

Conor put the basket on the stainless steel surface of the self-service checkout and immediately a voice came from the machine. It sounded like the same woman who did the Argos dial-up service over the phone. She had a nice voice, Conor thought, English but not too English, but she had pronounced Dun Laoghaire 'Doon Laharr', although someone must have complained because the next time he rang Argos she said it right. The woman asked him to place his items in the bagging area, then asked Conor to scan his items, then said – ten euro ninety-four. The screen gave him the option of buying a bag. He checked how much money he had – not enough to buy one –and pressed 'own bag'. The woman thanked him for his custom and the machine proffered a receipt. Conor squeezed the items he had bought into the bag holding his internet magazines and left the shop.

He wouldn't make any fuss. He'd take his dinner upstairs to his room when he got home; he was sure his mother would have left him something under the grill. He really hoped the house would be empty when he got back. His phone alerted him to a new Facebook notification then two. He checked it – *Gerry Donovan commented on a photo that you're tagged in*; and a message from Dave Coleman – *Wanna meet later Temple Bar*. He didn't want to go back into town to meet Dave. It was getting to be more and more of a strain with him. Dave liked to push things too far with the drink.

There was no one at home. His mother had left a note to say she was across the road in Rita's house. Up in his room Conor felt a satisfied click in his head when he turned on his computer. The screen lit up. He put the reheated Chicken Tikka Masala – which his mother had left for him under the grill – on one side of his computer, the Diet

Coke, bags of fun-sized Mars bars and one of the chocolate Swiss rolls on the other. Then he sat down, humming an echo of the reassuring musical signature of the start-up as he lifted a large forkful of Chicken Tikka Masala to his mouth.

Clicking on the movie-making programme, he realised that something wasn't right. The programme brought him into an earlier version of the project he had been working on the previous night. All the new stuff was gone. He clicked on the History icon and in Documents and looked in Search Programs and Files in case he had saved the new material under a different name, but nothing could be found. He searched under Downloads and in Conor's Stuff. Why had he not saved it? Then he remembered having been distracted the night before by a photo which came up in the small Facebook window with a message that simply said 'Hey you! Long time. What's up? A girl he had known at college, Alexis Auger, and how sexy she'd looked in the photo and how surprised he was that she'd sent it to him as a private message, and then he'd wondered if she'd really sent it to him or had someone else, pretending to be her, sent it instead. He remembered the irritation he had felt at that thought and how he'd then gone to the kitchen to get something to eat. He must have somehow shut the computer down before leaving his desk. He checked the computer again. He hadn't saved a thing. Jesus! He couldn't believe it. He felt the tears well up in his eyes and a hard lump rising in his throat and he wanted to smash the wall down, he really wanted to, he really did. He had spent hours at it, hours, and now he'd lost everything.

The doorbell rang. Conor chose to ignore it. Bound to be children calling for Halloween treats, he thought, the hard lump still in his throat. Though perhaps it might be his mother, having forgotten her keys, which she often did. He'd better answer. He moved slowly down the stairs and opened the door. Standing on the doorstep was a group of five girls, aged around fourteen or fifteen, dressed in next to nothing. They were squirming from the freezing night air or, he could imagine his mother saying, from shameless impudence and they all wore heavy make-up. One girl had a pair of devil's shiny red horns on her head. The girls rubbed their shoulders up against each other as they laughed. 'Trick or Treat,' the tallest girl let loose, like a bucket of cold water had just been thrown over her. The other girls cackled and screamed and arched their backs and then pouted their huge, red lips and looked very seriously at Conor.

He was about to say that he had nothing to give them when the girl with the devil's horns said didn't she know him from somewhere and wasn't his brother Oscar Mannon from Newpark and didn't he go out with her oldest cousin and hadn't her cousin thought Oscar was real good looking and so had they all, and they all laughed at this and elbowed each other. Conor nodded politely and smiled at their affected coyness and said, yes his brother was Oscar and he tugged at his T-shirt. The smallest of the girls who wore the least amount of clothes said that it obviously ran in the family – good looks – because he wasn't such a bad looker himself. And the girls laughed again and bit on their huge red lips. And although Conor thought that was an odd thing for the girl to say, he felt himself blush nonetheless and the hard lump in his throat softened. He apologised to the girls, saying he had nothing for them. The girl with the devil's horns said they wouldn't go away until he gave them something, because after all it was Halloween and they'd made a special effort to call at his house. And Conor, feeling his mood lifting in response to their carry-on, smiled again and said he'd give them a Halloween treat only if they sang something first. They all turned and looked at each other wide-eyed, their mouths stretching in the same rectangular grimace. Go on! said Conor, and he thought about Marika and how much she had enjoyed having a laugh with him. The girl with the devil's horns nudged the smallest one who made a face as though she was seeing a ghost. Conor playfully said, I'm waiting, and so the smallest girl began to sing:

> C'mon baby make my dreams come true
> Work me, big boy, do that thing you do
> Give me hell, smack me up real good
> You know I want it bad, I know you want it too.

She sang with a serious rock-pop shimmy to her voice while the other girls stood there silent and shivering. As the smallest girl sang, Conor found himself joining in with her, as he knew the song from a link on Facebook:

Work me hard, bad boy, play your dirty game
You the best, big boy, with all your money and your fame

The smallest girl suddenly stopped singing but Conor continued, his voice gallant and quavering and tiny-sounding in the cold night air:

I'll give you hell, I'll smack you up real good
I know you want it bad, you know I want it too.

When he finished, the girls said nothing but cast their solemn eyes down to the ground. Conor told the girls to wait and he went to get some apples and some fun-sized Mars Bars. By the time he returned a thin drizzle of rain had begun to fall and the girls' shoulders were hunched and their heads were bowed. Conor handed the apples and the Mars Bars to the smallest girl. She didn't smile or say thank you, but instead asked him what was on his shoes. Conor looked down. The edges of his white runners were covered with a sticky brown substance. He lifted one foot, then the other, and saw that the same sticky brown substance was crammed into the grooved soles of each runner from his walk across the stretch of wasteland on the way home.

—It's clay, he said.

—It looks like shit, said the girl with the devil's horns on her head.

—No, it's clay, he said to her, lifting his head.

—Well … it still looks like shit.

The girls moved off. As they reached the end of the short driveway of Conor's house one of them shrieked: OH MY GOD *he was sooo creepy* OH MY GOD OH MY GOD!!! The other girls laughed as they spilled onto the street.

A Painful Case

Paul Murray

Mr James Duffy lived in Chapelizod because he wished to live as far as possible from the city of which he was a citizen and because he found all the other suburbs of Dublin mean, modern and pretentious.

J ames Duffy, restaurant critic, was the most feared writer in Dublin. His reviews were infamous for their brutality. 'For mains, I ordered the steak tartare,' he wrote of Rumpole's. 'However, the waiter must have misheard me, and thought I asked for a giant pus-filled herpes on a plate.' 'Is there such a thing as a chicken Auschwitz?' he wrote elsewhere. 'If so, could I ask La Coupoule to please stop sourcing their birds there?' (This had generated a record number of complaints.) He excoriated both the humble ('Punjab Palace's beef curry is like a twenty-minute bout of the Ebola virus') and the very grand ('The great Dostoyevsky said that hell was the suffering of being unable to love. However, he hadn't tried the lamb at Zazie's.')

The proprietors of these restaurants protested that James didn't understand their food. They questioned whether he even liked food. It was true, he had no background in cuisine, whether *haute* or any other kind. He'd started at the paper as a music critic; the restaurant column had been his editor's idea. But while he might not know anything about food, he knew pretension when he saw it. When James was growing up, there hadn't been any restaurants in Dublin. Now the city was rich and everybody knew everything and eateries had sprung up everywhere, temples to pleasure where you could go and worship your own insatiable appetite. The excess and the self-congratulation made James sick and he said so. His uncompromising style brought him a large following, and his columns were read by people thousands of miles away from the Dublin dining scene.

His editor said that James was an ascetic sort; he said he could imagine James in medieval times walled up in a draughty monastery, going blind over a page of illuminated manuscript. His house in Chapelizod had the same white walls and bare floorboards in every room, and apart from his sound system, his weights, and a few rudimentaries, there was hardly any furniture. Unless he was reviewing, he stuck to a low-carb diet; tuna, protein shakes, that kind of thing. The day after his restaurant dinners he'd feel heavy and nauseous, and as soon he filed his copy he'd hit the gym until he'd burned off every calorie of whatever shit he'd had to swallow, then go for a run in Phoenix Park, which adjoined his neighbourhood. If it was late, it'd seem like he had the whole place to himself, apart from the herds of deer that cropped the moonlit fields. But in isolated spots he'd find lone cars parked, and as he ran up the wooded road past the Magazine Fort, he might meet a flustered, embarrassed form emerging out of the bushes, or a pair of dark eyes questioning him from the leaves. Sometimes, if he was in a bad mood, he slowed his pace, daring one of them to proposition him: he imagined his quick fists lashing out through the dusk, a split-second of surprise crossing the stranger's face before his body crumpled to the ground.

The weakness of people repulsed him, their pitiful hunger to belong. They didn't care what kind of lesioned meat they put into their bodies if it meant they could escape their own loneliness for a minute or two. James didn't believe in loneliness. Everybody was alone, was born alone, died alone: deal with it. He lived without companions or friends, just like he lived without religion and politics.

The one indulgence in his life was music – specifically, the US hardcore of the 1980s, Fugazi, Soulside, Minor Threat, those guys, the godhead for James being New Jersey band Maximum Outrage. In his gym, he'd hung a framed photograph (the only picture in the whole house) of the band's singer, M.O. Maxtone, at a gig — crouched at the edge of the stage, bellowing into the crowd. Sweat cascaded from his shaved head; the mic was gripped tight in his hand like he was choking it to death. About a third of the picture was taken up by his arm, so bulging with muscles it seemed on the point of exploding. Every square inch was covered in tattoos — a sun, a skull, stern commandments from Sun Tzu and Nietzsche, right on the bicep a stark black string of letters that read SS.16.7.64–12.1.82. Contrary to what some people believed, 'SS' was not a fascist reference. It referred to Maxtone's best friend and former bandmate, Steve Sands, murdered on the street by a crack addict in Sinico, NJ, the town where the two men had grown up.

Sands's death had been a turning point for Maxtone. He vowed never again to waste a single second of life. He gave up drugs, alcohol, television, every dumbfuck stupefacient society hands out to keep us narcotised. Sex too: sex was the most insidious of all, a self-produced opiate that enslaved the body and the mind. He described his celibacy as a never-ending fight with an invisible enemy. Every time I mastur-bate instead of touching a woman, he said, I do a good thing for myself. Instead of letting his strength be leached away, he directed it back into himself — honing his mind, taking up weights and making his body at once a lethal weapon and an unbreachable fortress. How different he was to the men and women of James's city, surrendering to every passing craving, endlessly glutting themselves like pigs at a trough!

James could still remember the first time he'd seen an Outrage video, that exhilarating feeling that at last he'd found someone who understood him. He'd taken up Maxtone's code straight away, and his friends of the time had done the same. They'd even started their own hardcore band, played gigs in the city. But the first thing you learn when you begin the journey of self-actualisation is that you have to make it on your own. They called themselves straight-edge, but all James's bandmates wanted to do was get wrecked and score the brace-faced teenage girls that hung around after the show. Eventually he got tired of the hypocrisy. He broke up the band, cut off contact with any of his friends whom he judged false or weak-willed or lazy or inordinately driven by their appetites. That accounted for everyone he knew.

He didn't mind being a restaurant critic; he enjoyed sticking it to those fat cats. Still he wished sometimes he were writing on a subject he actually cared about. He'd asked his editor if he could write some record reviews on the side, but his editor felt that would dilute the brand. You're getting a thousand times more hits now than you did with your music column, he told James. Literally, a thousand times more. So James kept going to the plush overheated rooms, kept eating the gussied-up cuts of dead flesh, the mi-cuit of foie gras and tiny bowls of pigeon tongues. 'Dessert was a novel twist on Pandora's Box,' he observed of the Chancery, 'in which all of the world's evils had been baked into a souffle.' 'Have you ever wondered what Hitler's heart might have tasted like?' he wrote of Huit Clos. 'Then the beef bourgignon is for you.' He once found a bullet in his soup. Another time a chef came after him on the street with a meat-cleaver. As he typed up his reviews, he imagined his fists sinking into the flabby bellies of the diners. His page-views went up and up.

One day his editor called him about a new restaurant. 'You're going to love this,' he said.

The restaurant was called St Tacito's; it was run by an order of monks. Monks? James repeated. I know! his editor guffawed. And get this, they've taken a vow of silence!

No one answered when he called the number, and they didn't have a website, so one evening James drove over on spec. The restaurant was way out on the southside, halfway up the Dublin mountains; he took several wrong turns before arriving at a pair of tall iron gates. Passing inside, he wound his way through a dark grove of trees and came at last to a building resembling an old schoolhouse. Its grey facade was stern but not unfriendly; yellow light poured out from a doorway where a man in cassock and sandals greeted James with a bow and an inquiring expression. So they really were silent! Feeling inexplicably foolish, James asked for a table. The monk tapped at his wrist and flashed his hands at James three times. 'Fifteen minutes?' James said. The monk gestured at the expansive grounds surrounding them. 'All right,' James said, rolling his eyes. He gave his name and phone number to the monk, then set off to explore.

It was one of those tricksy summer dusks, when the twilight makes everything look like a stage-prop, at once insubstantial and laden with meaning. Wandering through the trees, James came upon a beehive, then an orchard; beyond, he found a topiary filled with leafy animals, and a flourishing vegetable garden. When at last his phone rang he had quite lost track of time. 'Hello?' he said. But of course there was only silence from the other end.

This time the monk brought him downstairs to a long, low room and passed James over to a younger man with a beard, who steered James to a trestle table at which several people were already eating. 'Aren't there any private tables?' James asked with twinge of alarm, but the monk didn't respond. He seated him opposite a man with a dickie bow, passed him a handwritten menu, then withdrew to a discreet distance. The menu listed one dish only, carrot and sweet potato pie. James motioned the monk back over.

'Am I missing something?' he said.

The monk shook his head.

'You don't have any starters? No specials?'

The monk gently pointed with his pen to the sweet potato pie. 'Fine,' said James sardonically. 'I'll have the pie.' The monk beamed and bore away his order. James shook his head in disbelief. This was beyond amateur. Was there even a point reviewing it? He was about to put on his coat when the monk brought over a small basket of bread. It was surprisingly good, warm and moist and yeasty. Chewing, James relaxed a little, raised his eyes and looked around. The low hall was full, but the atmosphere seemed different to the usual ostenta-tious clamour – quieter, calmer. Maybe the serenity of the monks was rubbing off on the diners. Above his table was a plaster statue, a robed man with a beard and a halo.

'Tacito of Tres Cantos,' the man with the dickie bow, who James had been avoiding making eye contact with, spoke up from across the table. 'He was a Spanish nobleman, captured by the Saracens while travelling in the Holy Land. They tried to make him renounce Christ. So he bit out his own tongue. Hence the vow of silence, you see. The monks believe that speech is a vanity that distracts them from God.'

'How about opening a restaurant?' James said. 'They're not worried that will distract them from God?'

'They're trying to raise money to repair their bell-tower. Once they have enough, the doors will close again. Until then, we have a rare opportunity to sample their famous cooking!'

James had never heard of their famous cooking, but when his pie finally came, he was shocked. It was as if you could – he struggled interiorly for the words – you could taste the *life* in each ingredient: you could tell that these were things that had grown, from seeds, in the earth. 'Good, isn't it?' twinkled the man in the dickie bow. Yes, it was good; digging into his plate, James felt a kind of glow, the same kind he did after a session at the gym.

The bill didn't come to much; it would take them a long time to get their belltower fixed at this rate. James left his card on the little saucer. After a moment, the bearded monk reappeared, with a concerned expression.

'Is there a problem?'

The monk pointed to a sign he hadn't noticed before, pinned beside the stairs: WE ARE SORRY, WE CAN ONLY TAKE PAYMENTS IN CASH.

'What?' James said. 'Why didn't you tell me earlier?'

The monk looked contrite.

'I don't have any cash,' James said, becoming angrier as he felt his face go red. 'I don't know what you expect me to do.' The monk nodded humbly. There did not seem to be a contingency plan in place; he just sighed and shrugged fatalistically, like a farmer watching a flood take the harvest.

James, who'd been readying himself for a confrontation, found himself wrong-footed. 'I mean I suppose I could send you a cheque,' he said grudgingly.

The monk's face lit up. He clasped James's shoulder, grinning and nodding, and as if everything had been resolved he lifted James's coat from the chair and motioned him into it. Now James was positively confused. 'Don't you want my address? Or my phone number?'

Evidently this had not occurred to the monk. He considered it for a moment, then waved it away. James was confounded. He took a long look at his silent interlocutor. The man didn't *seem* like a halfwit; he was around the same age as James himself, with grey flecks in his beard that complemented intelligent grey eyes. James wondered what had brought him here, imagined some mystical, bell-like summoning of a kind that James would never know. 'Thank you,' he called after him as the monk withdrew; then he climbed the stairs towards the star-laden sky.

His editor called five minutes after he'd sent in his copy. 'I don't get it,' he said.

'What don't you get?' said James, though he knew.

'Did you even write this?' the editor said.

'The food was good,' James said. 'I'm allowed like somewhere once in a while, aren't I?'

He'd meant to ask his editor to post out a cheque, but the annoying conversation drove it out of his mind, and it was nearly a month before he remembered that he'd never paid for his meal. He tried calling, but no one picked up; feeling bad for abusing the bearded monk's trust, he decided the best thing was to drive over himself with the money.

This time, as he passed through the gates, he noticed the bell-tower the man with the dickie-bow had mentioned. The upper half had totally collapsed, and the remnant was shrouded in weather-beaten netting. Though it was early in the week, he found the dining hall almost full. The same monk was waiting tables – of course he was, he lived here, James told himself. He went over to him directly and handed him the cheque, apologising profusely. Far from being angry, the monk seemed not to think the late payment even an issue, and invited James to stay and eat. Tonight they were serving a leek and parsnip gratin, garnished with beetroots, hazelnuts and goat's cheese. ('You have goats here?' James said. The monk pulled up a sleeve to show a large bite-mark on his wrist.) Off-duty, James did not linger over the subtleties of flavour; he ate quickly, and when he was done sat back against the wall and let a pleasant feeling of tiredness wash through him. As there seemed to be no hurry to get him to leave, he ordered a coffee, then took out his laptop and started doing some work. Before long he was so engrossed that he'd quite forgotten where he was, until a fresh cup of coffee materialised at his elbow. James pulled off his headphones and raised his hand. 'Uh, I didn't order this,' he said. The monk made a munificent gesture: on the house. James was impressed. Most Dublin restaurants didn't give refills, just one instance of the secret meanness that lay beneath the shows of luxe. 'So you guys really never speak?' he asked the monk.

The monk shook his head.

'Really? Never?'

The head shook again.

'Wow,' said James. The monk bowed, then made to go. 'I'm a restaurant critic,' James said impetuously.

The monk stopped, and nodded, though it seemed more out of politeness than anything else.

'In fact I reviewed this place a couple of weeks ago,' James said. 'Gave it quite a good write-up – you've probably noticed it being busier.'

Again the monk smiled graciously without seeming actually interested. Talking to someone who'd taken a vow of silence was hard, James thought – knowing that everything you said, no matter how clever or insightful, registered first and foremost as noise, the same empty clamour they were trying to escape. It was a shame, because he suspected the two of them might have a lot in common with regard to their views on the vanity of the modern world. Regretfully, he fell silent, but instead of leaving the monk paused, and pointed to James's headphones, from which a dimunutive racket still poured. 'Maximum Outrage,' James said. 'You know them?'

The monk laughed soundlessly and shook his head.

'Like a shotgun to the face,' James said, quoting Lester Bangs. The monk raises his eyebrows. 'Probably the best rock band that has ever existed,' James said. 'If you want I can burn you a CD.' As soon as he said it he wondered why. Could monks even listen to music? Other than hymns and so on? But the waiter seemed touched; he bowed deeply, hands pressed together. 'I don't know your name,' James said. 'To send it, I mean.' With a smile the monk pointed to a white curl of scrip that still lay on a platter on the table. 'What? Oh, Bill? Bill, is that you?'

The monk chortled silently.

'Bill,' James repeated with satisfaction, and with a glad heart he mounted the stairs.

He gave a lot of thought in the days that followed as to what he should put on the CD. After trying out several different playlists, he finally decided *Bile Beanz*, Outrage's first album, was the best place to start. Maxtone recorded it when he was eighteen; Steve Sands had been murdered only a few months before, and the pain was audible in the singer's voice. *God is dead / and I envy him*, he screamed over and over on the title track. James smirked to himself, wondering what the monk would make of this.

A few weeks later, he was in the area, so he called by the restaurant for dinner. It was busy, but as the crowd thinned out Bill came over and thanked him for the CD, miming a package being opened and his face lighting up. 'What did you think?' James asked. 'Not exactly *Songs of Praise*, is it.'

The monk's smile dropped, and for a moment he just looked terribly sad, as if he were viewing an animal with a terrible injury that he didn't know how to help; and James felt a strange chill inside.

He returned to St Tacito's regularly, eating there once or twice a week. He'd usually arrive late, and talk to Bill while he cleared the tables; later, if there wasn't much to do, the monk might sit down with him. In the beginning, their conversations were casual. James would tell him about the latest restaurants he'd been to, the latest gourmet trends, and Bill would nod along. As time went by, though, he found himself wandering into other territory – art, his family, growing up in Dublin. Bill always listened keenly, whatever the subject, and because he never commented one way or the other, James was able to expand or digress or start talking about something else as the mood took him.

He couldn't quite pin down what it was about Bill he liked so much. The other monks were as serene, or serener. Yet with Bill there was a sense of hidden depths, of past struggles and victories hard-won. James would try sometimes to coax him into revealing something of his own life, but he never pushed too hard. He had had his own years of confusion and directionlessness, no doubt, but what was the sense of asking about it? When you had come to a point of enlightenment and understanding like Bill had, you probably didn't think of your old self as even being you. He seemed to exist outside of time, away from the idiot flux of events.

Still, James couldn't understand why he would bury himself away in a monastery. 'What's the point of it?' he said. 'Don't you get tired of praying all day?'

The monk laughed soundlessly, and made an expansive gesture with his hands, stretching them wide apart, as if describing an enormous fish: which James took to mean, There's a lot to pray for. That was all very well, James said. 'But what good does it do?'

If the monk was offended, he showed no sign of it; he simply shrugged, and smiled at James, as if to turn the question back onto him. What good did writing vitriolic restaurant reviews do? Fair point, he conceded.

James had never had what you'd call a mentor or a confidant; most human communication was in his view either procrastination or mind control. Yet talking to the monk he felt his thoughts grow in a new direction. Things that had been confused became clear; things that he thought were sturdy he realised had hidden flaws. Though Bill never spoke, his presence was a kind of field that transformed what came into it, and over time James found Bill's way of thinking entangling with his own. When he was alone he wondered what Bill might be doing, imagine him bent over a little black missal or lying flat on a board with his hands folded in sleep. Though he did not and would never believe himself, it seemed he could imagine the God that Bill believed in; and with that thought came a new and unknown peace.

'What the fuck is this?' his editor said.

Five minutes earlier James had filed a review of Lachapelle's, a French restaurant helmed by a notoriously difficult chef.

'He's not difficult, James, he's a white supremacist. He's gone on record with this shit.'

'The food was good,' James replied, feeling guilty, then angry, then tired, all in a moment.

'No one wants to read the food was good,' the editor said scathingly. James made no reply.

'Your hits are way down,' the editor said.

James knew his hits were down. He knew the readers were unhappy. Lately he couldn't motivate himself to hand out the drubbings as he had before. The floundering attempts at sophistication just struck him as sad; making fun of them suddenly seemed sterile and pointless. What had it achieved, his three-year campaign of vitriol? The restaurants were as busy as ever, the patrons as smug and as spendthrift. What was the sense of making himself angry just to please a bunch of readers he'd never met? Who were they anyway, these anonymous multitudes, administering their 'hits' with such fickleness? Were they any different to the thoughtless porkers that chowed down at Guilbaud's? Sitting at their computers, reading his articles for free as they skived off work, looking for a momentary diversion from their own barren lives?

Lying in his bed that night, James realised he had come to a turning point. If his mission was to wake the world out of its stupor, then it had failed. He could rail and inveigh all he wanted, it wouldn't change anything. People just didn't react to that kind of rhetoric. If you wanted them to think differently, it had to come from inside. Look at Bill. Without arguing, without saying a single word, he had rendered James's thoughts more intense, more impassioned, more truthful; just by being himself, he had taken James past the rote mockeries of his column towards something bigger. If only James could do that for his readers! If only he could show them what Bill had shown him! If only he could bring Bill to them!

He was half-asleep; this thought arose and slipped by like all the others down the drowsing river. It was only a few seconds later that a bolt of electricity seized James's body and pulled him upright in the bed.

'I thought I might bring someone along to dinner this time,' he said to his editor the next morning.

'Okay,' his editor said.

'Maybe someone with their own opinions, that I could bounce ideas off.'

'Sure, whatever,' his editor said.

'Might help to get a fresh perspective.'

'Do what you want,' his editor said.

As soon as he'd put the phone down James set out for the monastery, feeling a nervous elation he hadn't experienced for years.

It was early, and the iron gates were still closed when he arrived. He had to honk the horn until someone appeared and let him in. There was the same pantomime at the main building. The door was opened by smaller, older man, who squinted at James suspiciously. 'Is Bill here?' James said. The scrawny monk scowled, then shut the door. What was happening? Had he gone to get him, or? Why couldn't these fuckers speak? James hovered on the doorstep. Minutes dragged by; in his stomach his nervousness soured into irritation. Birds twittered in the trees, cassocked figures stooped over the vegetable garden; into this idyll the ruined belltower jagged gruesomely like a broken tooth.

At last the door opened and Bill appeared. He was covered in sawdust, and looked surprised to see James. With a mouth that had suddenly gone dry, James began to present his idea. But what had seemed so clear on the way over now turned into babble, so he gave up, and simply asked Bill if he wanted to come for dinner the following night.

For the first time, James saw Bill thrown. He stroked his beard and nodded to himself, but he avoided looking at James; and as James stood there, the manifold absurdities of his plan danced in a chorus line before his eyes. Bill was a monk. He had entered a monastery because he *didn't want* to go out to restaurants any more, or to cinemas or bowling alleys or whatever other alleged attractions the world offered. Even if he did want to, how could he leave the monastery? Wouldn't that be jumping headlong into modern vanities?

As Bill, plainly uncomfortable, hemmed and hawed, James began to blush. What was he doing here? What did he really want from Bill? A slice of his peace, was that it? Was he hoping to suck up some of Bill's tranquility, as if the monk were a scented candle from the New Age shop in the mall?

But wait – Bill was smiling. He pointed inside and up with his thumb, then weighed his hands in an imaginary scales, but finished with a thumbs-up, as if to say, *I'll have to run it by some people but it should be fine.* Then he took James's hand and held it in a firm grasp, and held James's gaze with his own, his eyes the colour of battered steel: and James thought that perhaps Bill understood what he wanted better than he knew it himself.

That night James was so excited he could barely speak. Already he had the article half-written in his head. At first glance, it would look like just another restaurant review, but then the reader would find himself brought into Bill's presence, and partaking in something much bigger, something enriching and noble and fine, just as James had been. Maybe there could be a whole series, meditations over dinner on various social isses, they could call it *The Punk and the Monk*...

The same scrawny man met him at the door of St Tacito's next evening, and scowled at James even more fiercely than before. Bill, however, glowed with excitement. He was wearing the same brown habit that he always did, but he had trimmed his beard and wore an expression of unalloyed happiness, seeing which James couldn't help but break into a smile. After a comical muddle of handshakes they bundled each other, laughing, into the car.

By the time they passed through the gates, though, the laughter had faded. For some reason the silence in the car seemed different than it did in the restaurant – pressurised, volatile. Maybe it was because they couldn't look at each other, James thought; or maybe Bill was nervous. When was the last time he'd been outside the monastery? 'Did you have any trouble getting out?' he asked him, but Bill just shrugged, and from the side James couldn't work out what it meant. He switched on the radio, but after a moment switched it off again. He didn't know if monks followed the news; he didn't want to deluge Bill with the world's woes. Though at the same time, why should Bill be exempt, he thought with a flair of irritation? Just because he believed in God it meant he could stick his head in the sand? He turned the stereo back on, and started playing the CD he'd been listening to on the way out, Maximum Outrage's third album, *A Painful Case*, which they'd recorded right after Maxtone got out of prison following a two-year sentence for assault – some heckler at a show who'd been shouting out bullshit about Steve Sands and in James's opinion deserved everything he got. The title of the record came from the prison psychiatrist's evaluation of Maxtone. Bill sat through it stony-faced, the furious noise smashing against his inscrutable silence all the way into the city.

As soon as they entered the restaurant, however, James felt his sense of purpose restored. Grey's of the Green was long-established, but had been recently revamped to capitalise on the *haute cuisine* gold rush: oak wainscotting, sequinned throw-pillows, flock wallpaper, mirrored ceiling, all thrown together like a cross between an Edwardian drawing-room and a Tallinn brothel. Amid the luxury and decadence, Bill in his simple brown cassock was a jarring sight. The coiffed heads of the diners turned to stare; James stared back at them defiantly, proud to be at the side of this singular man.

The menu was hopeless, a mess of meaningless adjectives and Frenchified jargon with no unifying idea beyond the profit motive. On the other side of the table, Bill seemed ill at ease, glancing about at the overcooked furnishings, the suntanned phonies and their Botoxed wives with an uncharacteristic wariness. James began to wonder if this was a mistake, if he should have chosen somewhere more laid-back for their first outing together. Still, when the waiter came to take their order, Bill went for the one dish on the menu that sounded in any way promising, a lamb tagine with orange zest sauce. James chose the wine, a decent-sounding midlist Barolo. A moment later they found themselves alone.

'Well!' James said. Bill smiled brittly, and unfurled the cutlery from his napkin. He seemed tenser than ever: his eyes kept flicking back to the glass of wine the waiter had poured for him. It took a moment for James to work out what was wrong, and then he laughed at his own thickheadedness. 'I'm sorry,' he said. 'You're probably not allowed to drink. I never even thought. Look, if you want, just leave it. Normally I don't touch the stuff either, except my editor thinks for a review it's important.'

Bill nodded seriously, considering this. Then with an *ah well* shrug, he lifted his glass, sniffed it, rolled the liquid up and back; he sipped it gingerly, and set it down with a little gasp of satisfaction. After that – as if Bill had at last given himself permission to be here – the mood lightened. His shoulders dropped, the old magnanimous light returned to his eyes.

The food, when it came, was better than James expected – or rather, it felt churlish to critique it when they were both having such a good time. James was telling Bill stories about his editor, various disastrous situations he'd got himself into after running out of coke; Bill was laughing and laughing, a fuller, richer laugh than James had heard from him before, that came from his past, perhaps, before he bound himself up in silence. The more he laughed, the more James's memories offered themselves up to be told. James was overcome by elation. It seemed he could feel some rusty hinge grinding within him, some great slab of a door swinging open. He signalled to the waiter for another bottle of wine, then smiled at Bill, a little ruefully. 'Ever feel like you've gone about your whole life wrong?' he said.

Bill's chuckles wound down and he gazed at James across the table. 'I just mean,' James gestured at the table, the plates lying between them, 'what's the point of eating a meal alone? Some things are meant to be done together, and that's that.'

Bill chewed thoughtfully, not taking his eyes away from James.

'It's not something I ever even wanted for myself,' James said. 'I just kept doing it because nothing better came along. Or I couldn't imagine anything better coming along. I'm starting to wonder if I'm stuck in a rut.' He looked up frankly at the monk. 'Don't you ever feel like that? In the monastery? Like it's not necessarily where you ought to be any more? It's just easier?'

Bill had stopped chewing: his blue eyes contemplated James expressionlessly. 'I suppose the thing about being alone is you get too far away from people to even remember what you're missing,' James said. 'It's like if you're wandering around the North Pole for years you stop knowing you're cold. Until, you know, someone asks you to sit down at the fire.'

He had never spoken like this to anyone; listening to himself, James wondered if it was the wine making him emotional. Yet nothing he said felt untrue. From the other side of the table, Bill was giving him a curious sort of look. Maybe he thought James was mad; James didn't care. 'I'm going to start doing things differently,' he said. He grinned at Bill. 'And it's your fault.' He lifted the bottle, emptied it into their glasses. 'I'm not going to remember a thing about this meal,' James said, 'we'll have to come back for lunch tomorrow.' Bill laughed; for a moment he seemed on the point of saying something, then he shook his head and addressed himself to his tagine.

Night had fallen. The restaurant's chandeliers glittered in the windows. James ordered dessert, then a coffee; then a dreaminess overtook him, and he followed his friend into silence. Perhaps silence was the true destination of any conversation, he reflected. So often our words get in the way of our real thoughts and feelings, complicating them and entangling them, when all we want from anyone is to recognise the fact of us! He felt that Bill recognised the fact of him; with a sudden surge of emotion, he thought that Bill might understand him better than anyone.

After the meal he drove Bill back to the monastery. Technically speaking he was well over the limit, but his mind was clear as never before. The car pushed through the night; like a river the city flowed over and around them. James felt that everything he had ever known was rearranging itself in his head, reconfiguring itself into a single crystalline truth.

Yes, being alone had a purity to it. But ultimately, wasn't it an impotent purity? How could you fight, walled up in your fortress? Maybe to achieve total self-actualisation you needed other people; you had to find the few select personnel who truly shared your vision and would help you to embody it. Even Maxtone had his band, after all, had Sands as a guiding spirit.

In the passenger seat, Bill's face was turned to the window. Light gleamed and receded from his beard, his robe; then, as they passed through the gates of St Tacito's, he fell into shadow. Looking at him, James suffered a momentary pang of sorrow, almost of guilt, like he was leaving his child back into boarding school. But this place was what made Bill Bill, he reminded himself.

The restaurant had closed, no lights were on anywhere. He pulled up a little distance from the main building, turned off the engine so as not to disturb the sleeping monks. In the darkness the world seemed far away. James sat there in the silence a moment. He felt exhausted and renewed, as if he'd just returned from some epic pilgrimage. He turned to Bill to thank him for tonight, and for everything else – there was so much to thank him for he couldn't find the words, so he just smiled bashfully. Bill, uttering a soft cry, leaned over to kiss him.

For a moment James could not comprehend what was happening; he was paralysed by the rush of alien sensations – the labial pull, the scrape of Bill's beard, the heat and smell and density of him bearing down on top of him. Then raising his hands he levered him off and pushed him back, kept bundling him though Bill was now back on his own side, till Bill popped his seatbelt, fumbled open the door and half-stepped, half-fell onto the grass. Adrenaline flashing through him,

James jumped out his own door and rounded the car. 'What the fuck?' he exclaimed.

Bill was half-crouched with his hands to his nose, dark liquid pumping through his fingers and onto his dark robe. 'What the fuck?' James repeated.

'I'm sorry,' Bill said – he *said*, he spoke, his voice through his fingers adenoidal and high.

'Sorry?' James shrieked.

'I thought …' Bill began, then stopped.

'You thought what?' James demanded. Closing in on him, he shoved his shoulder. 'You thought what?'

'You kept talking to me!' the monk protested, in a voice high with anguish, throwing his bloodstained hands about. 'You kept coming out here, and then tonight, when you said – you said you'd been living a lie –'

'Living a lie?' James repeated incredulously. Bill was gazing at him again, his eyes large and stupid and full of hope, as if this might be no more than a crossed wire, as if James had momentarily forgotten his own feelings. 'I've been lonely too,' he said, taking a step forward.

'Shut up,' James warned.

But Bill kept coming, kept babbling on, in a nasal Midlands accent James would never had imagined for him, a shopkeeper whine redolent of penny-pinching and mediocrity – saying that for a long time now he'd been having *doubts*, he'd been wondering whether he was cut out for the monastic life, and then James had come along and put these very thoughts into words, James by his presence had made the answer clear, had given him the courage he'd been missing – as though overcome by his own words, he came at James again, his arms outstretched –

'Stop!' James brandished a fist, his heart like a fist clattering against his ribcage.

'I know what it's like to be afraid of who you are,' Bill whispered.

The punch sent him careering backwards, leaving him sprawled out on the grass. He wheezed and sobbed and James stood over him and listened to it. He had never hit anyone before. He was surprised at how satisfying it felt. Blood throbbed in his ears, and his muscles, his lungs, the mighty engine he had turned his body into hummed with exaltation: he realised for the first time what it was for. From the ground Bill looked up fearfully and raised his hands for mercy. They were covered in blood, and black clots of blood flecked his beard. He looked weak, and old. 'If I see you again, I will kill you,' James said.

A light had come on in the main building. He turned away from the stricken man and went to his car. As he opened the door a voice cried from the grass, 'You have to let someone in!' James started the engine, wheeled the car about, and as more lights came on and the monastery door was thrown open, he sped back down the driveway.

The review he submitted for Grey's did not mention a dining companion. It launched a series of columns of unprecedented savagery. Yes, his editor said, this is the good stuff!

James did not see Bill again, but he thought often of him and of how grievously he had misjudged him. Silence, it turned out, was no less deceptive than words. Silence had enabled the monk to present himself as quite other than he was, as someone strong and wise and good, when in reality he was no better than the porcine wage-slaves at their gilded troughs. He was worse. At least they didn't pretend to be anything different than what they were. Bill's whole life was a lie. He knew what he was, but he didn't have the courage to admit it; he had spent his days on the run from himself, hiding out like a common criminal. Until James came along! James came along, and it all came slobbering out, the same dismal disastrous egotistic wantings as everyone else. God, that voice! That awful wheedling pleading voice!

Things changed in the months that followed. After his string of hatchet jobs, some restaurants announced they would no longer serve him. Initially James's editor was delighted by the publicity, but the newspaper's owner began to worry about libel actions, and as more and more restaurants joined the boycott it became clear that James would simply no longer be able to continue in his job. He didn't care; he was sick of the whole business. He called his editor and told him he wanted to quit. His editor said he just needed a holiday. Then he proposed that the newspaper *send* James on holiday. One of those package deals. Afterwards you could write about it. You in fucking Benidorm! He was laughing already.

James was dispatched to a resort in Spain. Bars lined every street, the ground was covered with puke and half-eaten kebabs. People fucked on the beach in broad daylight. At night, they pounded on his door, fucked in the corridor outside his room. James felt like he was the last one of his species. He experienced a hunger, a literal, physical hunger for a single word not slurred with alcohol or ignorace or obscenity.

On the plane home he was the only person who took a complimentary newspaper. The other passengers had been drinking since dawn. They ran up and down the aisle, propositioned the air hostesses, roared and guffawed in unison. The air was rank with farts. James put on his headphones and opened the paper and towards the back of news section read a story about an Irish monk who had committed suicide by hanging himself from the rope of a recently-restored belltower.

The air hostess was speaking to him. 'You're going to have to take those off, sir,' she said, pointing at his headphones. 'We'll be landing shortly.'

'Oh,' he said, doing as she told him.

'Didn't you want your meal, sir?' she said, taking the tray away without waiting for his reply.

In the seats behind him a group of men started singing football songs. His eyes would not focus on the page, the story came to him in fragments. Middle-aged man, struggle with alcoholism, statement from the abbott, restaurant now closed. Ex-wife, three children.

The men cheered as the cabin lights went out. This was normal procedure as the plane began its descent, the hostess explained over the PA. If you wanted to keep reading, a reading lamp could be found overhead.

James folded the newspaper closed and turned to the window. As the plane banked the lights of the city came into view. That black mass in the middle must be Phoenix Park; it seemed he could see himself, tracing lonely circuits through it, while down by the Magazine Fort men waited in the trees for someone to recognise the fact of them, to hold their bodies against the cold earth.

The city wheeled drunkenly. The men behind chanted and sang. One by one Bill climbed the steps of the tower. No, James said aloud, but Bill couldn't hear. From the wing the landing gear whirred and chunked into position; the air roared; Bill stood at the edge of the darkness, the bright new bellrope in his hand. For a moment everything stood still. James pressed his hand to the glass, as if he could touch him. Then the ground hurtled up towards them. Ladies and gentlemen, welcome to Dublin, the air hostess said. Somewhere he heard a bell ring out, a single, sustained peal of surprise and hurt; then the sound died away and silence, sweet silence, prevailed once more.

Ivy Day in the Committee Room

Eimear McBride

Old Jack raked the cinders together with a piece of cardboard and spread them judiciously over the whitening dome of coals.

L ately they came in from night, lustrous as dead dogs on the turn. As fat with air and cinder-eyed. Jack, alone, bony in the injudicious light of a long unserviced flame. Patched pimply since life's handiwork undid, Mr O'Connor rolls himself a cigarette, makes a cylinder of some lot's gawdy pamphlet, lights, and sets it all a go.

—Did she say when Tierney'd be back?

—She did not.

Leg stretched and meditative O'Connor follows

—How's your young fella?

—A boosing bollocks, like the rest of them these days.

—The young have no decency anymore and can't have a finger laid on them.

—I tell you, if I was my father, he'd be booted from here to kingdom come. I wouldn't mind but he and that mother never wanted for a thing.

—What age now?

—Just the nineteen.

—Risky enough age these days…

—Worser in our time.

—Speak for yourself. At least then it was ferries instead of the graves and this one doesn't look like going away.

—Not any time soon, Jack concedes Is it me or is this shower the uselessest yet?

  O'Connor havers, then gives the fake coals a belt.

—Come on you pup! So… will you be out the twenty-seventh?

—My canvassing days are done.

—I never thought I'd hear you say that.

—Me neither but they have us all strapped and mashed and I'll be damned if I'll wave a flag too.

—God, do you remember that night?

—I do and don't expect to see its like replicated any time soon.

  Steadfast in this Jack resettles himself. O'Connor martyrs his cigarette but turn they both like stomachs in the face of a morning-after day.

—Hi, what are ye lot doing sitting here in the dark? Would you ever switch on that light!

—Arragh Hynes, how goes it?

—Pestering, in that awful fucking rain.

  Jack fixing a two-eyed clamp on the scut sliding in, asking

—Any sign of Lord Lucan of Lucan? while demystifying his floaty bronze specs.

—No, fecks O'Connor like sarky 'as if'

—What do you think Jack, will he reappear? Or has he hopped it?

—Mmm, gives Jack craw Much the same as that Colgan.

—He was barely a bricklayer.

—Hand in glove's what I'm saying.

—If I knew then…

—Oh then you'd have known a lot and not be left goggling the high-tailing spondulics.

—Fare thee well to the good auld envelopes, for they have gone their way.

—Not everyone was on the take.

—Not everyone no, but we're all getting chilblains.

—Well whatever else, I'll give Tierney this, at least he wasn't up on the podium kissing the good queen's arse.

—Arragh! Arragh!

And quivers the flame in swipes of

—What difference does all that make?

—Once it would.

—Once generations of mess and it doesn't even matter anymore.

—It matters.

—It matters to *who*?

—No, *who* matters is where we are now.

—No, we're at who matters to *you* because the country's hardly watching at all.

Tinter into silence and draws of cigarette.

—As well this is a club boys or ye'd all be out in the wet!

Blue hand rubbing and busying 'bout little chill-eared Henchy comes in.

—No Jack don't shift, I'm grand. O'Connor, did you approach the wife?

—I did, yes.

—And?

—She said to check Aungier street.

—And did you?

—I did, Grimes hasn't seen hide nor hair these passed two weeks.

—Jesus! How did he manage it, the prick!

—Because he was 'Tricky Dicky Tierney' and we paid no heed. Now off tanning his hide while we choke on the broke fire he had rigged.

—That's all very well but...

Unsoftly breathed.

—Did we know?

—Did we know?

—Sure we knew.

—Like his father before, oiled for the ready, then through!

—Well if he thinks I'm finished...

—What will you do?

—I'll...

—You'll hope and wait and when the time comes, open your door to the bailiffs.

—Ah now Hynes...

—Uncalled for...

—Maybe gents, and since there's no new news, I'll be on my way then.

Chuckles and chortles till he's out through the door, when Henchy turns

—What was Hynes here for?

—Ah leave him, he's weirdo but a decent enough skin.

—He is not. I'm telling you that maggot is spying... The neck of him asking Did we know? What we'll do? Then he's off to what he's salvaged for himself alone while the rest of us have to go skulking along. And as for the bailiffs... where did he hear?

—So who d'you reckon he'd be spying for?

—Who? Anyone! Take your pick. You can't spit in this city without hitting a grievance.

—That's true and him the lickspittle he is.

—His father turning in his grave. Silken Thomas isn't in it.

O'Connor alone, rolling again, rolls against the swim.

—Do you not remember though, how he used to be? Madly fervent about it all... Stepping out of the Imperial shadow... The democracy of it... Us taking our place. He's bitter now about the way it went and us getting jingoed up.

—Still...

—Still...

—He was wrong.

—It never made us a people, like the loss of it does.

—And now at least we're back on home turf!

—Ha and fucking ha.

Knock on the door.

A Father afoot. In new priest grey. Collared. Blue shirted. With the approachable face of the fallen from grace but a smile for them nonetheless.

—Oh Father Keon, come in come in.

—Don't mind me, I'm just chasing young Mr Fanning.

—Black Eagle these days, but won't you sit?

—If he's not here I won't not disturb you.

And re-ascends he off out into the flapping black. Undisturbed and at cigarette suck they let him off the hook.

—What is he?

—They, you mean, what's all them these days?

—Mostly, I'd say, bestridin' a bit less for fear of troubles they hope we won't seek.

—But he wasn't...

—Not that I heard...

—And how much does that mean?

—Ha ha, you have it. And have you noticed, of late, how they're hovering us up again now the money has fled? They were biding until we were shamed to the knees.

—Where we've always liked it – if memory serves.

—It's not memory they'll be likely to poke.

—No, they'll stir the stick in your throat that the money kept good and relaxed.

—Bad years for them.

—Just the start of deserved.

—They're a set of Kitty's...

—And on that note so, can I wet my throat with anything else?

—There'll be plenty once we're servicing our dues again, according to the jippy wee shit down below.

—No.

—No!

—I'm afraid, yes.

Ah, tsk and eye rolls.

—Send to the Black Eagle then, they won't have the face to turn us off.

So O'Connor makes fingers out the door while Henchy expounds on his schemes of Office – from whence he'd ride those forgetful rats right round the place.

—Knowing tons, as they do, about how to lay waste by lashing away at the poor, old and helpless to keep have for the haves like they should.

—Haves?

—And were not we then?

—No!

—That was never meant… that was never the idea at all.

—We were for the nation.

—And ourselves.

—And the euro.

—And the fall at the end of our own fear of fall, which lead to a fall… and a fall… to a fall to a

Knock!

—Okay, the young fella says.

—There's a few bottles there but he says not to expect, not anymore. He's not his brother's keeper or the cellar for the CR.

—Does he now and what else does he say?

—That the pub's started circling the lip of the drain so all ye vultures can go to hell.

—Still he sent this?

—For historical conscience he did.

—Well pass round them glasses. Ah cork! Shit!

—Don't worry, I've my Swiss army knife with.

—Have a drink for that so.

—Don't mind if I say yes, and he downs it all in one.

—How old are you?

—Seventeen.

—So, what's next then?

—I don't know… something… somewhere…

—A ticket?

—A plane?

—Can I be bothered?

—Have another.

—That's how it begins.

—Ah Jack, you know his liver's probably already twice as big.

—And is that to be proud of?

—Is just now and ever been.

—Better a day with than without, laughs Henchy. Especially mine, going pillar to post, tracking dockets to nothing and dodging the phone.

The youngster, relying on life for his hope, tufts his hair up and scoots on out the door while the drinkers' mouths break down their wine and long around for more.

Soon knock another and the door boots in.

Crofton!

Advances over the room in the burl of his worth.

—Where's that wine from?

—Trust you.

—Always can! peeps Lyons – ushering in like sucked dust behind – To be pounding the streets while youse warm yer behinds. Give us a glass of that.

—The young lad's gone with his knife.

—Fear not! Do you know this trick?

—Which?

Soothing the neck, Henchy thumbs its cork back in.

Pfungk!

—Now that's a good one!

—Don't ask who taught me it, nudge wink.

Twists each then with the tricks that they know and their stink. Recalling to mind what greats there's been and how arid it is since those broad years of slipping – recollections and hands out of sight. That burgle for burgle's sake opening life into velvet for chancers. Scoring so high on the wants of a people surprised at being able to get for a change. At being able to open their mouths and say Yes.

At shrugging off lives most formerly possessed of patience and not much more. *Pfungk!* Oh we wheedled them right to the gorge. *Pfungk!* Only now we must coddle them back, fuck it, dolled-up in our ashes and sacks. But we'll abide too in patience-sheathed suits, observing them waking their own over-reach. *Pfungk!* Keep unobstructed their in-turning gaze. Careful in public not to delay the inevitable clothes-rending call to regret. What's a change ever but sorry for it? No, from our Pale of red tape made, we will watch their bruises fade. And live to fight another day. New Ireland's dream all along.

—Pass another bottle of that putrid wine.

Pfungk!

—Hey look, back again Hynes?

Hynes nods

—Crofton, Lyons. I saw you passing so... any news?

Crofton declares

—He's definitely gone.

—Is he really?

—Where?

—And when?

—What does it matter to us beyond he cleared out all his bank accounts? Now's the time to start digging in.

Smirks Henchy

—'Romantic Ireland's dead and gone'

—Christ if I hear that one more time...

—More like 'Come gather round me, Parnellites' Jack groans.

—No, Hynes says I've a poem.

Then clears his throat to others' Go on, and neat fold-handed begins.

> Bertie brought a bit of butter,
> But the butter it turned bitter.
> when Bertie bagged all the better butter
> to keep his bitter butter better.

Slump in the room around them. This day gone all the way down.

—Well I think we should leave it at that. Not much point in

162

reconvening I'd say either, lads. So, unless there are any objections I declare the Committee Room is done.

There's a rise at Jack's formality but no voice goes awry. Glasses slip onto the mantelpiece. One last glimpse cast for old time' sake as the pilot light gives up its ghost amid sunk cigarettes. Then go these crossed and double men out into the Dublin night.

—Crofton, what day is it? asks Hynes, on the step.

—What?

—What day is it?

—Sixth of October... or seventh...

—No Crofton, what day is it though?

—Jesus Hynes, I don't know.

A Mother

Elske Rahill

Mr Holohan, assistant secretary of the Eire Abu Society, had been walking up and down Dublin for nearly a month, with his hands and pockets full of dirty pieces of paper, arranging about the series of concerts.

Ger, chairperson of the Gaelscoil na Cnoic Naofa parents'
committee, had been bustling about the clós and corridors
for almost a month now, her head swivelling about doorways and
her expansive round haunches stuck out behind her like an ostrich's
plumage. She held a clipboard and made vague enquiries and vague
requests, pulling the laminated photograph out of her bum-bag and
telling anyone who would listen about the Brides Again evening.

But at the end of the day, it was Kathleen who arranged things.

'If you're going to do it,' Kathleen's mother used to say, 'do it
right,' and, to elaborate on this advice, 'If you want something done
right, do it yourself.' These, Kathleen thought, were the best pieces of
advice her mother had ever given. She tried to teach her daughters the
same thing, to drill it into them, so that they would come to expect
it of themselves, so that they would be ashamed to be late or to only
half-do their homework.

When she was twenty-nine, Kathleen had married urgently out
of practical good sense. She had spent her secondary school years

at a convent boarding school. (She would have sent her own girls there too, only it was closing down next year.) Despite being a prefect, sporty, thin in her youth, despite having the resources and the taste to dress well and behave properly, and despite going to the races with the more popular crowd at school, Kathleen had never made good friends there, and when the Leaving Cert was over and all the girls dispersed, she found herself alone.

Some of the girls went to UCD, but Kathleen had taken an events management course at a private college. She was a good-looking girl back then, with caramel highlights in her hair and a high pony-tail. She worked out twice a week at the gym and went for a swim every other day. The worst her enemies might say of her was that she could be a little insipid-looking, if she didn't highlight her hair regularly and colour her face in with make-up. But the few boys enrolled on the course were scrawny and unambitious, and she graduated at the age of twenty-two with only a handful of disappointing cinema dates behind her.

Still, she did not lose heart. Even if she could be pale sometimes, and her lips not very full, she was very presentable. She knew how to dress and how to walk, she was never caught without well-manicured nails – things like that mattered in her line of work. Straight after college she found herself a good position at PARTY PRO, managing their corporate gigs. She was good at the job, and was given ever-greater responsibilities. She liked the big events. She enjoyed wearing the name card around her neck, using the walkie-talkies, and arranging people. She enjoyed her own fierce efficiency, and liked to say 'imperative.' 'It is imperative that everyone be in their places for seven …' she would say, or, 'You are late. It is imperative that we have a team we can rely on!' She began to make an effort with the men she met at work, but none of them were very impressive. Many tried to start something with her, but never with the sort of passion or adoration she had hoped for from a lover.

She began to worry that there was not, as she had been raised to believe, someone for everyone. She soothed her bouts of panic by walking for a long time on the treadmill in the gym, her high pony-tail swishing reassuringly to the beat, and sometimes by eating large amounts of Turkish delight in bed while watching TV. The intense romance she had once imagined looked less and less likely, as she began to fatten around her hips and under her chin.

But, as her mother would say, Kathleen always had great get-up-and-go. When she heard that three of the girls from school were getting married that year – and had not invited her – Kathleen took great joy in surprising them all by sending out generous wedding invitations. She would marry Graham; an accountant at her father's firm.

He was much older than her. Until recently, her mother had explained, he had been dedicated to a woman who suddenly married someone else. He had no children. She had hoped to marry a solicitor – that had been her mother's secret ambition for her – but she knew she had to be practical, and, according to the nice suit he was wearing, and her father's familiar attitude with him, he was good at what he did. He had kind lines on his cheeks. She liked his clean, oval nails and the gentle way he passed the salad bowl that first evening when he came to her parents' house for dinner. By the time the leg of lamb came out she had made up her mind. She smiled at him softly over the pavlova roulade, and said that she never drank anyway, so she could drive him home. A year later he took her to dinner one Friday evening and asked the waiter for his best champagne, before proposing calmly. After eighteen months of co-ordinating, the wedding day went off without a glitch.

She had never quite given up her romantic notions, though. Sometimes, if she was very early collecting the girls from school, she would read novels about true and forbidden love in the car before going to wait in the clós. They were about affairs between rich ladies and working men, or romances set in Victorian times with the sex tastefully hinted at, or sometimes she read racier ones where women made men weak for them. And sometimes, but not often, when the girls were at school and the au pair was out, she climbed into bed with a small wooden box of real Turkish delight – translucent, sugar-dusted little cubes of emerald green and red, which she popped into her mouth whole – and watched a DVD with Colin Firth in it …

But she made sure to be a good wife. She always had his coffee on when he woke. She prepared a wonderful meal every evening. Even years into the marriage she continued to have her hair highlighted, and she always took the time to look after her skin. She understood that the little things mattered. When Graham had a work do, Kathleen was always the most attractive and well-dressed wife in the room, and she knew Graham appreciated it by the way he introduced her: 'my lovely wife – yes, I know, she's a little out of my league!' She could engage in good conversation with his female colleagues too, having been a career-woman herself. 'I was a career-woman myself,' she would laugh, '… in a previous life!'

Kathleen once found a brown envelope on a shelf in Graham's office, in amongst his books. It contained cards and letters and odd little keepsakes; a paper hat from a Christmas cracker, train tickets, a piece of ribbon. There were photos in there too, of the woman he had loved, who he never spoke about. It comforted her to see that the woman was far fatter around the middle than she was, and it looked as though she had bad skin. Nonetheless, there was one photo where Graham was smiling at the woman in a way Kathleen had never seen him smile.

She had made the right decision, though, marrying Graham. Her first impression had been spot on – he was a decent man through and through. It took them seven years to conceive. They had all the tests but still the doctor couldn't tell them why it didn't happen. Kathleen kept it to herself. She knew people would suspect – she suspected it herself – that it was her coldness that was to blame. She hadn't the warmth, perhaps, the passion, the integrity to make anything grow in her. Graham kept it all very quiet just as she asked. She knew that some men shied away from all the investigations, but not Graham. He attended all the tests and meetings and funded every treatment without question. He was a good husband and a good father. And he had his head screwed on. He researched the property market and didn't take big risks – they hadn't been hit as badly as some by the recession – and he looked after his daughters, saved for them, planned ahead. When Cliona was born, it was he who had suggested the au pair to help Kathleen with the housework, and she had to admit she enjoyed how the other women envied her when she mentioned their holidays in Portugal and the South of France. Not package holidays either. 'My Graham,' she would say, worrying sometimes, even as she spoke, that the girls would find the familiarity of her tone incongruous with the grey-faced man they had met, who, even after twelve years, still nodded at Kathleen politely, and looked through her like a stranger when she told him things about her day, 'My Graham insists on doing it right. A villa in the South of France, he says, or nothing at all. And I have to confess … it is just *gorgeous!*'

Kathleen had said to Graham before, though, that they would encounter problems if they sent the girls to a non-fee-paying school, but he wouldn't listen. He was all about saving their trusts for college and sending them to the Colaistes. The Irish second levels got the best leaving results, he said, and there was no point even putting the girls' names down, unless they sent them to one of the feeder Gaelscoils. No point at all.

And for a while, it had seemed as though they had made the right choice. Kathleen had put her best foot forward – *if you're going to do it, do it right …*

She had organised parents' mornings. She had helped out at the fundraisers. She was on the parent-and-teachers' board. Her eldest, Roisín, won the school Irish dancing competition two years running, and pretty little Cliona was invited to all the boys' birthday parties. It was Kathleen who always organised the gift for the teacher at Christmas and the end of the year, tactfully requesting only €5.00 per person – the rest she would chip in herself, and, of course, the teachers knew it. But there it was again – the same old problem. For even though the school professed to be Catholic (and they didn't all profess such a thing nowadays) and was situated in a good part of Dublin, there were children from broken homes in Cliona's class, there were families on social welfare, and even a little boy with long hair who belonged to a single mother. People like that couldn't be asked to chip in more than €5.00. So it was Kathleen who took the hit.

The single mother bothered Kathleen somewhat. It was her brazenness. She skidded about smugly in a battered little Fiat as though it were a Rolls, and stood in clós waiting for her lanky, bedraggled kid. She would lean casual-as-you-like against the wall, smiling away in her skin-tight mini-skirts and knee-high boots without a care in the world. The way she kissed her child as well, and tousled his hair, all sweetness and joy – you'd swear she was the world's best mum. That's if you didn't know that the poor kid had never met his father! Some of the mums said it was a married man who had fathered the child, and that was why he wasn't on the scene. People talked. The kid was bound to hear it someday, and what kind of life was that for a child?

As Graham had quite rightly pointed out, though, there were no non-nationals at the Gaelscoil. At least there was that. It wasn't a question of racism. Kathleen simply didn't want her child held back because Bubba Mac Zuzu at the Educate Together couldn't understand a word of English. That was fair enough, Kathleen thought, and the other mums all agreed.

In a way, it was because of the single mother and the broken homes that the whole idea had taken off in the first place. Kathleen had been in to talk to the muinteoir about it. She wasn't hugely religious herself, she said, but she went to mass, and, well, it was worrying, the things that Cliona was coming out with. Cliona said the long-haired kid had run crying to the teacher when Cliona told him that ladies couldn't have babies until they got married and prayed for one. 'That's not true,' he had said, 'My mam isn't married and she has me.' Apparently, whichever muinteoir was on clós duty had said sometimes that was true and all families were different and some Educate-Together, hippy-dippy, happy-clappy nonsense like that. Now, these muinteoirs were supposed to be in charge of the childrens' moral education as well. Cliona would be doing her communion next year, and that everything-goes attitude was totally outside the school ethos, as far as Kathleen was concerned.

Ger agreed. She said she would raise the issue at the next committee meeting. But when the day came, and Ger asked Kathleen to outline her concerns, some of the mums looked at each other under bowed heads, chewing their lips. Ger assured her she was taking the issue seriously, but her cheeks raged puce and she kept flitting off the subject all the same.

'Show me your friends and I'll show you who you are,' her granny Kath used to say, and sometimes Kathleen thought of this when she met with the girls. It was her duty as a mother, of course, to put in the effort, but sometimes she wondered if she should really be keeping company with messy women like Ger; disorganised women who dubbed themselves easy-going, who laughed with their heads thrown back and made jokes about their weight. Kathleen smiled politely at Ger's jokes – what else could she do? – but if she looked like Ger she wouldn't be laughing about it. Ger sometimes farted at coffee with the girls, and then chuckled. She made Kathleen feel prissy and pernickety.

And anyway it was all a facade – the easy-going thing. Ger had gone to a lot of trouble to have a new dress made up. That's how it started, really. During coffee with the girls Ger had taken a laminated wedding picture from her handbag and sighed before handing it around, 'Look what I found in the bits and bobs drawer! I'd never fit in to that dress now – would I girls?' The bride in the photo was slender with pink cheeks. Her close-mouthed lipstick smile was neither happy nor sad. And it made an ache in Kathleen's chest to recognise, in the little creases around her eyes, in the dimples, in the small hands; big, dough-faced Ger. It made Kathleen's stomach tighten so that she couldn't finish her latte.

That afternoon she had screamed like a banshee because the kids were laughing too loudly in the back of the car. She had noticed, in her rear-view mirror, that the blue lines under her eyes were worse than ever. When she got home she pressed fifty euro into Marillia's hand and asked her to take the kids to Wagamama and Leisureplex, even though it was a school night. Then she had climbed under the duvet with a few little pieces of rose-flavoured Turkish delight and watched the whole of *Pride and Prejudice* on the new wall-mounted flat-screen.

That night, while everyone slept, Kathleen lay looking at her husband's back. His skin was very white and there were a few sparse black hairs between his shoulder blades. He hadn't showered before bed, and his skin gave off a sour, oily smell. At 2am she crept down to the hallway and poured a glass of Chianti. She sat on the cold polished-oak floor with the glass and gazed at her own wedding snap, tastefully framed and presented on the hall table for all to see. She thought of poor fat Ger with the beautiful Thai au pair. 'Did she not have a photo with her CV?' Ruth had asked.

'I would worry,' Kathleen had said, 'about an au pair like that … does she go about in her nightie?'

'Ha!' Ger had said, picking up a mini croissant and pushing it through her pillar-box lips – and she a diabetic, 'I wish she would! One less job for me to worry about!'

It was that kind of attitude, of course, that lead to messy houses, poorly adjusted children, wandering husbands, but, thought Kathleen, but … That young, slim Ger in the photo, with the excitement in her cheeks, with her uncertain lips turned up very slightly at the edges, with the tense dimples and the disappointment already creeping into the corner of her eyes – hadn't she been a good girl, trying her best? Weren't they – all of them on the parents' committee – good women, good mothers trying their best? Staying married, staying faithful, staying respectable? What gave her the right – the young single mum – 'she's a researcher' Ruth had said as though she knew what that even meant – what gave her the right to swanny about in a rickety tin can and no trousers on, call her bastard Blaise, of all things, *Blaise* – to swanny about like Lady Muck as though she had no shame in the world with her wild black hair and her pert little ass?

Kathleen had spoken to Cliona. She had explained that some people weren't taught right from wrong by their Mummies and that those people should be avoided. The child agreed that the kid would not be invited to her magical-genie-and-bouncy-castle party in June.

What thanks did they get, people like Kathleen and Ger, for doing the right thing? Why did they deserve to feel unattractive and useless and petty? If it weren't for people like them there would be no parents' committee, no present for the teacher at Christmas. They deserved to feel excited and pretty again. They deserved to feel, every day, the way they did on their wedding days – like the most beautiful woman in the world.

In her wedding snap Kathleen sat with Graham in the vintage wedding car and they each held a champagne flute. It had cost a fortune, but Kathleen's mother had said you only get married once, and it should be the best day of your life, and her father had said he would spare no expense for his only daughter's wedding.

She had blond ringlets and she wore a tasteful half veil. Her smile was proud, as though she were receiving a prize. Kathleen tried to remember how she had felt when the picture was taken, but she couldn't even remember the photographer's name. She remembered the wedding night, when they retired to the penthouse suite. Neither of them was too drunk. She had been glad of that. She had searched Graham's eyes while she undressed and when he mounted her she had smiled and thought, 'I am as beautiful now as I will ever be.' She had smiled and searched his eyes and said, 'I love you' with all the passion she had imagined she would one day feel for her true love. She remembered feeling a fool, because Graham's eyes were the same after the wedding as before – of course they were – flat and mild and giving nothing away, looking at her bottom and breasts like a spectator, and her voice sounded ridiculous when she said it, 'I love you,' shaking her head slightly, with too much emphasis on the word 'love,' like an old-fashioned actor, and she had felt, just for a moment, that it was not she who had craftily orchestrated her destiny, but someone else. She had felt, just for a flash, when Graham's eyes shifted away from hers, when she said it again, 'I love you,' that she had been duped, that she had been made a fool of.

Ger went for the idea immediately. The others giggled but they wanted to do it as much as Kathleen and Ger. 'Just for the laugh,' Ger had said, and the others had blushed and nodded, 'just for the craic ...' That was one thing Ger was good for – getting people on board. She made them embarrassed to say no. Ger talked a lot, but it was Kathleen who had spoken to the priest and organised to borrow the red carpet from the chapel. Ger had a new wedding dress made, and so did Becky – exactly the same as the originals, but much bigger. 'If we're going to do it,' said Kathleen, 'Let's do it right!' But Kathleen didn't even need to alter her dress. Her body had slid easily into the cool satin bodice. The limousine idea was hers. She suggested a stretch limo to bring each of the Brides Again to her house for the evening. Every girl must have their own limo ride. Every girl must feel special. But then there were complaints about the cost. There was a recession on, they all said. Ger had already spent a fortune having her dress remade. Then there was the alcohol, the food, the babysitters ...

Kathleen's girls would be heading off with the au pair to Trabolgan; Graham would be away on business. It had all been planned for weeks. The business trip was a big deal. He had bought a new suit for it, and a new razor, and it was going to involve four days away. He would be back that night, but not until late. He probably wouldn't be there until after everyone had left. Brides Again was going to be a girls-only event. Kathleen suggested the Mummies had their husbands look after the kids – 'Don't we deserve one night, girls?' She had a great solution too, to the food cost. Each of the girls would bring the first dish they had made as a married woman. There were nine of them coming – Kathleen would make the canapés, Ger would be on entrées, there were two women on starters, three on main courses (one carnivore, one veggie, one gluten-free) and two on desserts. Then the only things they needed to chip in for were the champagne and the limousine. There had been no charge for borrowing the red carpet. 'It's a good cause,' the priest had said.

But there was coughing and muttering about the limousines. It was the usual suspects – Ruth, and the other one with grey streaks in her hair who never wore make-up – Gráinne. They said they'd pass on the limo.

'I think you might be going too far …' said Ger.

'Come on girls,' Kathleen said, 'if we're going to do it let's do it right!'

Kathleen suggested they could hire only three cars. Each car could make three trips and the cost could be split … Then Ger had to push it. It was too expensive. It was a silly expense. Out of pure desperation, Kathleen had suggested just one, it was much cheaper if they just hired one for the evening to pick them all up. The two stick-in the muds grumbled their consent.

'But each bride rides alone in the limo with a glass of champagne,' said Kathleen, 'He picks one up, and drops her, then goes to get the next one…we can start the canapés while we wait.'

Ger said she'd collect everyone's contribution and they would balance it all out at the end.

By the time the evening came it seemed as though it was all going to tick along nicely. Marillia's friend, another Spanish au pair, came to help for the evening. She did a great job cleaning the house, and decorating it with silver ribbons and white balloons. She spread the red carpet all the way down the hall and out into the gravel driveway. It seemed as though the limousine plan would be fine. Kathleen had asked all the girls to text their addresses a week before so that she could give them to the driver. Then she had called the limousine firm. She had organised a pink stretch limo. It was a little more expensive than the girls had agreed to pay, but Kathleen made up the difference.

While she waited, Kathleen walked about the house by herself in her dress and make-up. She found herself wandering into the hall over and over, and gazing at her wedding picture. All day she couldn't help thinking of something silly that had upset her last year. It was the kind of once-off glitch that all marriages have. The kind of thing she knew should be let go.

It was that time at the theatre. Graham was quieter than usual at the interval, staring into his glass after he had emptied it, tilting it about so that the ice swirled and clinked in the dregs. When she went to the ladies she understood. Standing in front of her was the lady from the pictures. She had, as Kathleen had rightly noted, a thick waist and pink spots under her skin, especially on her chin. She had felt Kathleen looking and she turned and smiled. She had something that Kathleen couldn't put her finger on; a brightness, a glint, and from her smile Kathleen knew that this was the sort of unbeautiful woman a man could fall in love with.

That evening in the car, out of compassion for Graham, she pretended nothing had happened. She chatted away about the play, and about their daughters, and she saw him flinch as though her voice hurt him. Then he turned to her suddenly, and rubbed his face hard, smearing his features and groaning quietly. 'Look I'm tired Kathleen,' he said, 'I don't care. I just don't care.' Kathleen couldn't remember what she had been saying, so she couldn't answer, but his face – the weariness in his voice – she felt a fool.

They drove home in silence. When they parked the car in the drive he said quietly, 'Sorry love. I'm tired.' Kathleen looked at her nails – freshly shellaced that morning so that she would look nice for the theatre. They were candy pink and she saw now that the colour was too young for her. She patted her husband's knee, 'Okay,' she said, and they went indoors.

Ruth arrived first. She and Kathleen ate canapés together in their wedding dresses for half an hour before Gillian turned up. Kathleen had asked her hairdresser to come out to the house that day. It had taken two and a half hours to get her hair right – with highlights and curlers and everything. She had contemplated getting a professional to do her make-up too. Standing by the canapés, the white paper table cloth flecked with pink and blue confetti and spread with seven different nibbles (Kathleen had made them all herself the night before, all from the first cook-book she had used as a new wife) she was glad she had done her own make-up. She had picked up a few disposable cameras in Boots, just for the laugh, and she asked Ruth to take some photos of her sticking her tongue out. Two hours later three more had arrived, but they were still waiting for one of the starters, one of the main courses, and the desserts. Ger turned up in a cab with a sherry trifle.

'Gráinne texted me,' she said, 'It was taking ages for the limo to get everyone, so we decided we'd speed things up and get cabs!'

Gráinne arrived shortly after, and then Paula, also in a cab. When the limousine finally arrived with Mary, Kathleen went out to tell him he didn't need to get the others.

She said it to him as though it was no great change of plan. He had been hired for the evening, and looked a little alarmed. But then he shrugged, 'Whatever makes the ladies happy ...' He asked what time he should come to pick them up. Kathleen went back inside to ask the assembly of Brides Again. When she entered the room they all stopped speaking and turned to face her. Ger held a champagne glass in once hand, and a blini with avocado and salmon cream in the other. 'Oh God,' said Ger, 'the poor guy. Tell him to go home. We'll get cabs.'

Two other Brides Again nodded and took large gulps of champagne.

'He's hired for the evening,' said Kathleen, 'We have to pay for the evening.'

There was silence in the room, except for the 'Here comes the Bride' instrumental that was still playing on a loop. Kathleen had wanted each Bride to arrive to that tune.

'I arranged to hire him for the evening,' said Kathleen, 'because that's what we all agreed.'

'I think we should leave it,' said Mary, 'we've had our limo rides now. I'd rather cab it ...'

They all stood around Kathleen's beautifully decorated dining room and looked at her. Each of their dresses was a slightly different shade of white or cream. Kathleen was sorry to notice that they all had too much rouge on their cheeks and each a different shade — some beige, some pink, some orange. She hoped her make-up was alright, and knew, suddenly, that they should all have chipped in for a make-up artist instead of the limo. She could have coordinated them.

'Perhaps he would do us a deal,' said Ruth, 'If we let him go home now?'

Kathleen touched her neck. She knew her lips had thinned into a straight cut, the way they did when she was angry. She had put a lot of work into this evening on the girls' behalf. After a little silence she said,

'Fine. Can I have the money to pay him please. €80 each, as agreed.'

'I gave mine to Ger,' said Gillian.

'Oh Kathleen,' said Ruth, 'Sorry, I forgot. Can I pay you on Monday?'

Then Kathleen heard Graham's car on the gravel outside. He came into the hall, sighed loudly and threw his overnight case on the floor. That wasn't like him at all. Graham was gentle and controlled in his movements. He placed things. He was never rough.

'Kathleen!'

'Oh,' said Kathleen, 'Strange. Graham is in earlier than expected.'

He came into the room and kissed Kathleen beside her mouth. 'Don't you all look great!' he said, and then, 'What's yer man doing in the pink limo?'

'Waiting,' said Kathleen, 'waiting to be paid as promised. But some of the girls forgot their money.'

There was a clustering about and a muttering. Ger went into the hall to get her clipboard and cashbox.

Graham smiled and shook his head, but Kathleen stood stock-still with a straight back and her hands clasped in front of her.

'I have gone above and beyond, girls. I organised the whole thing. I even paid extra out of my own pocket to get the pink stretch one – and not for myself. I didn't even get a ride in it …'

Ger came in from the hallway with Ruth and Mary and Gráinne, and pushed a crumpled pile of money into her hand.

'We'll give you the other €200 on Monday …'

'Well,' said Kathleen, touching her veil and the soft caramel curls, 'Well it won't do. I need to pay the limo man. And I need to be reimbursed for the champagne …'

'Oh Kathleen,' said Graham, 'don't embarrass yourself. Just use the card. Sort it out later.'

Kathleen rarely said no to her husband. She respected his authority on these kind of things. But she put her foot down on this one. 'No,' she said, 'no. Ger agreed to collect the money.'

She stood looking at her friends. They lowered their heads. Ruth picked up an entrée, and put it down again. When the driver came in to see what time to come back at, Graham hushed him out and, Kathleen later discovered, paid by card, plus 10% admin charge. Then he came back in and said, 'Yis look great girls! Enjoy. Just pretend I'm not here, I'm going straight to sleep!'

Kathleen tried her best to enjoy the rest of the evening, to be a good host, to put her best foot forward, as her granny Kath would have said. As they grew drunker the girls began to laugh and take photos. The food was cold with all the delays so Kathleen put it in the Aga for a bit, and then they all sat around the table in their dresses and rouge, and they talked about their wedding days, and their husbands, and how they had met them.

Grace

Sam Coll

Two gentlemen who were in the lavatory at the time tried to lift him up: but he was quite helpless.

Nobody could quite tell where Mr Vernon Crumb came from. Ostensibly Irish, and doubtless a longstanding Dublin resident, such surmises would be belied whenever he opened his mouth to speak. He spoke in a quick and rapid voice, fast emitting clipped vowels of no known geographical provenance (though the dominant notes were either Welsh or Pakistani). His quicksilver speech was often muffled and indistinct, and much of his incoherent converse could thus pass over the listener like a cloud. And his fluttery movements, augmented no doubt by the gallons of free liquor he daily imbibed, were jerky and unstable, making him seem like an unsteady puppet on the brink of collapsing when denied Gipetto's friendly guiding strings.

Courtesy of such a liquid diet of which he was vampiric adherent, his face was indeed very ruddy, the scarlet cheeks puffy and the flabby neck jowly, but more alarming still were his popping eyes whose roving gaze was furtive, their brows beetling, half hidden under lank strands of his greasy black hair, whose roots disclosed the silvery beginnings of grayness. A natty dresser whose dapper apparel recalled vanished days as a bygone dandy, he wore the same double-breasted suit and tartly glitzy tie for all occasions, such seeming sartorial elegance undermined by the seediness of his garments, unwashed and unkempt and wearing down to the very cloth. There was a rumour that he once had worked in RTÉ as some sort of sound engineer way back in the seventies, though if he had, that hardly mattered nowadays.

For jobless sixty-something Mr Vernon Crumb now firmly belonged to that class of persons known as '*liggers*', an admirably resourceful strata of society who chose to combat the city's mounting prices and the scarifying cost of living by frequenting reception after reception, and reaping bounteous fruit from this plentiful harvest. A kind of underground club had formed over the years, of which Mr Crumb was a founding father, though when it came to rallying the troops and planning the assaults, he admitted to being too scattered a personality to ever undertake such a responsibility, and so had yielded in supe-riority to one Conan Kelly, late of the Department of the Marine, an enterprising sort who had taken it upon himself to act as the free-loading army's ringleader. This Mr Kelly was ideally suited to his post, for he possessed an exhaustive knowledge of the town's freebies, and knew exactly where and when everything was on, courtesy of his privileged access to secret knowledge from undisclosed sources.

He had a select little list of his choicest friends, of whom the vener-able Vernon was one, to whom he sent out daily bulletins of the latest book launches, or exhibition openings, or gala receptions, or inau-gural lectures, right down to the afters of a college debate, keeping his comrades informed via a deluge of emails, somedays numbering in the tens of dozens. And it was a brave habit of theirs to constantly play the party's spares, sidling opportunely in just when the fun was about to begin, riffling some crackers and cheese from the plates, ignoring the angry eyes of the event's overseers as they stumbled forward with a wineglass for a fourth or fortieth refill, affecting not to notice the superior glances of sniffy disdain bestowed upon them by the snootier set who felt themselves better placed to be present.

Such familiar looks of subdued loathing greeted Mr Crumb this misty Thursday evening as he entered the college grounds and shuffled up the TCD Graduate Memorial Building's steps, whereupon he infiltrated the Philosophical Society's Common Room, where the bevy of tuxedos postured and milled, holding forth and keeping court in the wake of the weekly debate, which today had been all about abortion. It was a debate which Mr Crumb had had every intention of attending upon awaking that morning, but the earlier opening of an artistic exhibition on Leinster Street had in the end commandeered the greater share of his attentions. Several glasses merrier and his eyes were glassier as through swarms of students and senators he now snaked and trod and made straight for the table of treats on which were enticingly strewn many large and fulsome platters. And the maturer interloper calmly ignored the disapproving eyes around him as he greedily surveyed the plates of cocktail sausages, of smoked salmon and spiced beef, of oily olives and sweaty cheese; if anyone asked, he was merely a loyal graduate recently returned for a bit of 'fourth level education'.

And as he pilfered some crisps and pocketed some chocolates to line his stomach before the next mouthful of Merlot, an unsteady hand on his sleeve bid him turn to greet a younger member of his cortege, the tall and gangling Dermot O'Connor, looking splendid in his military jacket and Jamaican bolo, part-time plasterer and occasional landlord who was letting out his lodgings to a pair of Poles. With a stoned expression he embraced his elder friend, who shook him off and grinned.

'How was the debate?' grinning Mr Crumb inquired.

Dermot O'Connor could not answer this question. Mr Crumb didn't care. In any case, Dermot was much keener on boasting about his recent success in gatecrashing a press screening for the forthcoming film *Albert Nobbs*; he had claimed, picking the name of a random periodical right off the top of his head, that he was with *Totally Dublin*, and was chuffed to find that the Lighthouse cinema staff did not demand any ID from him to bolster his phony claim, and so thus did he swagger inside to enjoy a free glass of bubbly, plus the bonus of a free film into the bargain.

'Bravo. What was the film about?' Mr Crumb warmly wondered.

Dermot O'Connor could not answer this question. Mr Crumb didn't care. In any case, the eager Dermot O'Connor had a fresher fund of important information to relay: he had just received a textual tipoff from their chairman Conan Kelly, who said that the next opportune port of call tonight would be the Workman's Club on the quays, where upstairs a prestigious book launch was soon to commence, with a free bar and various other edible or drinkable amenities for the gang to enjoy.

'Sounds splendid. What is the book about?' asked kindly Mr Crumb.

But Dermot O'Connor could not answer this question. And Mr Crumb didn't really care. Instead, he passed the dithering pothead a weighty bottle of beer and asked after the condition of Dermot's tenants, who had apparently of late been giving Dermot much grief, which happy topic roused Dermot to vociferously vent his spleen on the score of his lodgers, spitting forth vicious flecks of beery froth from his flapping wet lips as he energetically cursed them, employing numerous unprintable expressions in the course of his eloquent casti-gation, manfully accepting Mr Crumb's muttered sympathies, token drops of empathy cursorily slipped in between pauses in his sips.

'Fucking polecats!' Dermot O'Connor spat. 'They have me by the balls …'

'This is it,' murmured Mr Crumb, demurely sipping his wine and licking his purpled lips.

And Dermot O'Connor angrily chugged and emptied his beer bottle he flung down with a snort and a belch. Staggering slightly on tipsier feet, he suggested they make tracks to their next location – for the present joint was becoming, as he said with a gesture to the timid crowd, 'a fucking drag'. And Vernon Crumb was only too happy to come, rapidly downing his glass with a final slurp and gasp. And so through the revelers they wove to the door, their departing backs enduring a last round of eyeball rolls and slighting shrugs as they hurriedly exited into the night.

As they quickly marched and felt the bracing breeze crashing upon their parched pair of drinker's faces, the swirling quayside air exhilarated Mr Crumb, moving him to attempt a twirl by the bridge's parapet as they waited for the traffic lights, gruffly bid desist in this potty pursuit by mortified Dermot, who remembered only too well a recent occasion when old Vernon had disgraced them all by repeatedly stabbing his madman's finger into a painted Adam's oily navel, rousing the wrath of the irate National Gallery guards who cared only for the precious condition of the desecrated canvas, and were in no mood to endure excuses of temporary insanity made on behalf of jabbering Vernon the crazy Crumb – they were bloody lucky to get off that time without a hint of litigation.

'Behave yourself!' Dermot O'Connor growled as they sidled into Workman's when her doors and gills were beginning to heave with the impending nightclub's throb, greeting the towering bouncer's scowl with lopsided smiles and flutters of flopping wrists. Grasping Vernon's elbow lest he should stray and give them away, Dermot steered him toward the stairs up which they unsteadily climbed to the fabled book launch, arriving in time to catch the very end of the publisher's speech, which mainly consisted of an invitation to partake of the booze and the biscuits, a gracious offer the pair of newly arrived inebriates were only too happy to gracefully take up with gusto. After each was armed with a wineglass, they swaggered to the bar and tapped the counter in command, and whiles their free and foaming pints were pouring, Vernon admired the wallpaper which was crimson and the lighting which was dimming, and was amused to note the name of the launched book in question – My Father, My Brother, My Sister, My Mother, a darkly comic deconstruction of the Irish misery memoir, as penned by a promising young author called Robert Cox. Dermot raised an arm to hail a distant stager lurking in a farther corner, none but Conan Kelly himself, squashed into a tight spot by the jostling flock who bought their books, looking squat and dumpy in his yellow raincoat on which his blue drool was drying, who saw Dermot wave, and awkwardly pushed through the crowds to meet his messmates.

'Hjgghj jngdrc ...' Conan Kelly slurred in salutation.

'Glad to see someone started earlier than me!' Dermot gaily beamed, lifting his glass to toast.

They drank, they supped, they downed, they sipped, they quaffed and laughed, they slurped and burped some more and further, between wine and lager and spirits and stout and ales alike they drunk like lords or judges. When heads were reeling and eyes were blearier, Dermot beckoned all out to the smoking section, into one of whose tighter recesses he lodged himself to roll a succulent spliff, which freshly smoking joint he gallantly offered to share with his colleagues, with the gentle proviso that they exercise discretion while passing around their prize to partake of furtive puffs, enjoying the mild elation offered by the crinkled weed, the queasy balm of soothing the gentle drag afforded, mingled at times with a soft qualm of worried regret over all the dross one wished to forget, beset by the fearful melancholy of all in life undone one always failed to do, the whisper of conscience that fretted the nerves and cast a frowning downer upon their superficial piece of peace.

Vernon Crumb was especially affected. His mind grew dizzier and his sights were swimming. Unhinged, untethered, he floated unnoticed away from the company of his unheeding friends, having a mind to go to the toilet, grasping hands pawing the brickwork as he swam through the dribbling rabble all around him whose clutches barred his jellied progress, groping through space in his wavering quest for the downstairs jakes, locating with strain the tenuous stairs down which he descended to the building's bowels, where the darker air grew colder and his bones were chilled. In the murk he was pointed to the pisser by a leonine lout, the path of whose scaly finger he followed until the toilet door swung wide open to admit his cautious passage, whereupon – he slipped.

He slipped and fell. He fell heavily, face first. The floor was wet; the attendant had been negligent. Vernon Crumb fell heavily and felt his face explode as he hit the toilet's tiles. His jaw made the hardest impact, feeling as if it were broken off. His dim sights filled to brimming with nothing but redness as bloody spumes blossomed from the wreckage of his crunched front teeth, and in a rapidly pooling circle of blood he lay and groaned and writhed helplessly on the damp tiled toilet floor, useless limbs quivering as cubicle doors were unlocked and a few spare sods at the urinal turned round to stare. And they gawked and they groaned and they roared in their rough pity.

'Ah man, had a few too many, eh? Jaysus, wooja look at that? Fucking ay!'

The hapless boys raised the alarm, and a trudging bouncer soon bound in, swiftly bending to roll the wretched man over on his back, suppressing a wince at sight of the crimson damage before producing a snowy handkerchief he clapped to the victim's mouth, gently easing him up and mumbling condolences as he struggled to stem the flow which showed no sign of ceasing. Dazed, Vernon Crumb attempted to speak but found speech impossible, having lost so many teeth in the accident that articulation was accordingly hindered. Dully he withdrew the stained handkerchief and marveled at the mottled imprint the discharge had left on its whiteness: it looked as though it had been dipped deep in ketchup, ketchup sprinkled by a cosmos of crystals of salt particles or sugar cubes, the cracked shards and disintegrated remains of onetime canines and smashed molars.

The bouncer laid a hand on his shoulder. The bouncer asked him his name. The bouncer asked him was he in much pain. The bouncer asked if he had any friends nearby who could help. To none of these questions could Vernon Crumb reply, reduced instead to a wetly incoherent flapping of his tongue, a low gurgling issuing from his throat. The sighing bouncer hoisted him to his shaking feet and propped him against the wall as he applied some searing bottled disinfectant to the emptied bleeding gums with dripping roots, gruffly snarling at the ogling boys to desist from their tactless sniggering scrutiny. In the meantime, his sympathy was soured when his nostrils caught a suspect scent emanating from the injured man's gaping mouth, an illicit hint of hashish such as enraged him.

'Listen to me now,' he said, pocketing the disinfectant and jabbing an admonitory finger in the wheezing victim's ribs, 'You're fucking lucky I'm not calling the guards. Now if you know what's good for you you'll just get the fuck out of here right now and don't ever dare come back.'

Vernon Crumb, his mind a fog and senses smarting from the stinging pain, yet had sense enough to comply with this suggestion. Wiping and mopping the ruins of his gums which still were leaking the last of his blood, with the glaring bouncer menacingly strutting at his stumbling heels, he painfully crawled upwards from the toilet's depths to the exit, staggering outside to embrace again the quayside air and cock a dull eye at the bright stars winking high above the chilly river. Some smoking strays took pity on the injured man who seemed so confused, and further questions were asked as to his identity and his destination and the location of his companions if indeed there were any, to all of which queries he gave the same impenetrable response with sad imploring eyes.

'Hong Hane!' he repeatedly hooted in mounting agony, his tongue tapping his lower set of surviving teeth, struggling to do the elocutionary work once done by his recently departed dentures.

An unknown young man in black stepped forward. He lived on Clanbrassil Street, and so may be said to have some knowledge of the surrounding terrain. Gently tapping Mr Crumb's shoulder, he asked if it was Long Lane the poor man meant. And his suspicions were confirmed when the enthused older man warmly responded with a stream of bloody spittle, accompanied by a few affirmative wags of the head, topped off by an attempt at a smile (no easy feat when the stock of smiling teeth was so depleted). This settled, the young man hailed a taxi, sharply directed the driver to Long Lane, and stuffed a wad of notes into Mr Crumb's hands, for all his mute protests.

'It's nothing. You just go home now and get some sleep, and go see your dentist at the nearest opportunity, y'hear? God bless and take care of yourself. Good night!'

The taxi beeped and sped off and the small crowd thereafter dispersed, the drama done.

While upstairs within Workman's, Conan Kelly and Dermot O'Connor were disgusted to discover that the bar's supply of free beer had run out, and the usual exorbitant prices were henceforth prevailing. And only then, as in a stormy huff they prepared to leave, did they pause to wonder over what had become of their poor vanished chum, the benign but batty Mr Vernon Crumb.

Margaret Magee preferred to be called 'Maggie'. She was a mousy old lady with stringy hair and little skinny limbs, warm hearted and placid, a love of wine being her one weakness. She had been a beauty once, a beauty confined these days to her eyes, and even they had begun to glaze with a whiskey's mist – no wonder she was on the fabled ligger's list. On Friday morning she checked her email only to find her inbox crammed with the customary thirty or so forwarded messages from Conan Kelly, strewn with umpteen invites for openings and announcements of upcoming events. Promptly, she texted Vernon Crumb to see to which one of these he was planning to come – for she could not be seen to freeload alone – she was something like the glamour girl in their boozy gang – and poor old Vernon was her especial favourite among the males – rumour had it that they had been an item once, way back in boozy days of lover's yore. Whether or not this was hearsay, the extra degree of fond affection existing between them today could not be denied – and so she was suitably alarmed when his illiterate reply gave her to understand that he was grievously ill and could not go to anything. Wary for her beau's welfare, she took herself to his house at once, resolving to be nurse.

He answered her knock with reluctance, unwilling for her to see the state to which he was sunk. With burbling tentativeness he opened the door a crack and saw her waiting on his doorstep, and his beady bloodshot eyes met her own dewy lovelorn gaze awash with concern, and he hummed and hawed before stepping back to admit her into his desolate Long Lane lair. She gasped at the sorry sight of him, haggard in his bloodstained pajamas with his face in a swollen mess, purple cheeks purpled further by a medley of greenish tinged bruises, chips of dried blood flaking off amid the grizzle of his stubble, opening his mouth ajar in a leer to display his empty row of nibbled gums, toothlessly grinning in wordless reply to her flurry of worried queries, raising a palm to entreat her be hushed, before miming a slip and a crunch through the gruesome pantomime of his witty fingers.

'O Vernon!' she cooed in concern as she swooned, 'You poor thing!'

Manfully he shrugged it off, indicating with a sweep of his hands that it was all as nothing, hinting with a wave that she need not be worried, but she wouldn't hear of it: she would be mother. She put him to bed and tucked him up, fluffing his pillows and brushing his hair and tending to his cuts with ointment and plasters, eyeing with maternal disapproval the disarray and squalor of his seedy bachelor's bedsit, tartly tut-tutting at the dust and the dirt she took upon herself to sweep and scrub. She tore apart his curtains and opened his windows to allow inside the sun and the air, sprayed washing up liquid on all the stains of his stove, then lit up the fusty hob to cook him up some soup, a gelatinous compound of whatever ingredients were to be found in the cobwebbed chaos of his cupboards. The broth cooked, she poured the steaming slop into a bowl and ladled it all into the gaping mouth of the bedridden invalid, wooden spoonful by messy spoonful, wiping his dribbling lips as he drooled and mumbled attempts at gratitude that she pooh-poohed.

Then she rang round the gang's other members to share the gruesome news and try piece together the sorry chapter of last night's cock-up, remarking on the wonder of how the poor man ever succeeded in getting home on his own while hotly berating Conan and Dermot for the negligent attentions they had shown him, not that they much cared or remembered. Finally she demanded that all come over for a conference in his digs, and decide how best to attend their fallen friend. He had always been erratic they agreed, but had of late been on a steady downward spiral, spinning out of control and indulging in outrageous public displays and whatnot, and this latest incident could mark but the beginning of the final descent. Clearly some sort of great lifestyle change should be put in motion; such an accident could well happen again, and next time he may not be nearly so lucky. And she implored them all to think over on how they could help, and to come armed tomorrow with sober plans and politic stratagems.

That evening she stayed on at Vernon's, sitting in an armchair by his bedside and comforting him with gossip, retiring to the couch to rest when he napped, awaking once or twice in the night upon hearing his muffled calls for assistance. And as a final reward for her matronly efforts, she indulged herself in a measure of spirits in the dullest early hours, a bottle of which she found secreted in a pouch beneath his bed. The stricken man's eyes lit up at the sight of the liquor, but she sternly admonished him to be a good boy and stay dry, for another drop was the very last thing he needed, as yesterday's mishap had shown all too clearly. He looked downcast, but kept quiet, content instead to watch with longing as the good lady poured herself a tumbler and enjoyed.

Conan Kelly was the first to arrive the following Saturday morning, looking shamefaced and sheepish for the part he had played in the debacle, yet also wobbling unapologetically on account of his breakfast beer, whose tang hung on his breath and gave Maggie to wince as she greeted him. As she took his coat and invited him to wipe the mud off his shoes, she warned him to be discreet when broaching the topic of temperance – the last thing they wanted was for Vernon to suspect a conspiracy, for he would never cooperate if ever he felt plotted against.

'Hyyhrj ggr,' said Conan Kelly – by which she understood that he would be tactful. To further assure her of the soundness of his aims and of the thoroughness with which he had thought things through, he dipped into his satchel and produced a pamphlet he passed to her with a meaningful glance: a disclaimer about AA meetings in Findlaters Church on North Frederick Street.

'O no, no, no!' Maggie Magee groaned, 'That's far too blatant. He'd be spitting. Really!'

Conan Kelly, his stratagem thus dismissed, shrugged and passed on in.

The patient sat up in bed and hailed his visitor with a throaty garble that really was no more inarticulate than Mr. Kelly's customary slurred gargle, his habitual mode of discourse. Pulling up a stool, Conan Kelly sat down by Vernon's bed, and pressed his arm and punched his shoulder, by way of bucking him up. Conan Kelly gave Vernon to understand that he was sorry that they had led him astray on Thursday, and expressed his hope that Vernon was in the process of recovery. Conan Kelly also assured Vernon that he was in very good hands. Conan Kelly also thought to inform Vernon of the gallery opening to which he was going that night, but then remembered that such a topic was taboo. In short, the company was warm but conversation was tough; Maggie was relieved to hear the bell.

Dermot O'Connor was the next to arrive, bowing his head and accepting Maggie's greeting remonstrations, bearing the chief burden of the blame on his own stoned shoulders, yet artfully omitting to inform her of the fateful joint he had rolled that night. He lumbered into the bedroom and slapped Kelly's shoulder, mournfully blanching at the sight of Vernon's injuries.

'Ah man, you're like a car accident!' he said jocularly. The victim simpered.

But after a warning glare from Maggie, Dermot O'Connor next chose to keep the mood determinedly light by recounting the latest sins of his resident Poles, the term of whose tenancy he was sorely tempted to terminate. All warmed to the subject, and for a time the matter of what to do with Vernon Crumb was put on hold. Then Dermot recollected his own contribution, and promptly took a card from his breast pocket and passed it across to Vernon, who accepted and squinted.

'My cousin,' said Dermot helpfully, 'Excellent dentist. Based in Swords. Really gentle, soft touch. Very high reputation. He'll kit you out with a new set in no time, mark my words.'

'Is he pricey?' Maggie anxiously asked, inadvertently squeezing Vernon's troubled shoulders.

'Oh well,' said uncertain Dermot newly crestfallen, 'Er, that's, uh, a good question … I'm sure he could, uh, do a discount or something if I put in the word … cousins are cousins, y'know …'

'Pprhg hugh,' said Conan Kelly darkly. All agreed, none more so than Vernon.

The doorbell rang again after some more minutes of painful banter, to Maggie's greater relief. The latest and last arrival was Mr. Martin Graves, a courteous and genial presence: Maggie's heart positively lifted when she first caught sight of him standing in the doorway, kindly smiling and crinkling his wrinkled brow as he offered her his hand, clasping her wrist with a feeling grip.

'Maggie,' he said warmly, 'How is he?'

'O Martin! It's a bad business …'

'We'll see what we can do,' said Martin Graves. And Maggie thought he sounded like a man who knew what to do. Mr. Graves, a well read and erudite man, was one of the later additions to the club, a former civil servant who had retired on account of high blood pressure and supplemented his pension by renting out his Phibsboro lodgings to a female couple who kept some cats. He had just returned from his annual autumnal stint on the continent, where he taught English for his keep and for his pleasure crooned elegies at the funerals of spinsters. For he had a fine pair of lungs and a tuneful voice that caressed the ranges both baritone and tenor, and in his heart of hearts he had always wanted to be a singer full and proper – it was through frequenting musical events that he had fallen in with Kelly's crew and had his email address appended to the grubby list. But though not impartial to a drop, he was a moderate man who seldom imbibed to excess; his friends among the freeloaders considered him something of the scholar of their set. They trusted his judgement and looked up to him for approval, often deferring to his opinion when debates erupted, whose outcomes he would chair. It was often remarked that his face looked very like that of Colm Tóibín.

'God bless all here,' he waggishly remarked upon entry into Crumb's dingy bedroom, Maggie following eagerly behind with yet another chair she set down by the bed. The atmosphere warmed as he lent distinction to the scene, resplendent in his tweedy suit and tie, and all around the bed shifted their seats to make room for the newest arrival, who casually accepted his natural preeminence in their circle. Vernon Crumb, who by dint of repeated efforts was now succeeding in stringing together tangible sentences, perked up to remark that Martin was looking very well.

'I thank you,' said Mr Graves, 'But I wish – no offense – that I might say the same of you!'

'Ah well sure, thish ish it,' said Mr Crumb.

'Now now, we've all been there,' said Dermot O'Connor.

'Please God but we have,' said Mr Graves with a chuckle, reaching back into his memory cabinet for the story he had concocted en-route for the occasion. 'Sure haven't we all overdone it at one time or other. Did I tell you the time about how I fell down some stairs in Spain?'

'You did not, Martin!' said Dermot O'Connor.

'Few years back. I'd had a good few on board, and, as you can imagine, I was a bit rough ...'

'Why!' cried Maggie, 'I never would have thought it of you, Martin!'

'... and I was coming home in the dark or something, dropped my key I must have, and in bending down for it I bloody well went head over heels down the steps. Cut open my arm, split my thumb and all – and it's lucky I escaped with just a slight bump on the head. I tremble to think what way it could have panned out. But as you can see, I'm still here. Not much to look at, but heh ...'

'O Martin!' cried adoring Maggie.

'That's a fine tale to be telling,' said Dermot O'Connor.

'Fj,bflk,' said Conan Kelly, wiping spit from the sleeve of his jersey.

'My thought exactly,' said Mr Graves, 'It's a dreadful habit and it will be the death of us all. But as the playwright says, it's a good man's failing. And from what I hear tell, old Vernon here has been behaving as badly as I did. You overdid it on Thursday evening I believe, did you not?'

Vernon Crumb reddened and shrugged. Mr Graves, weary of the inquisition, took pity.

'But it's no great sin to be merry. Sure what else would you do in the evenings, I ask you? Could one not go to the cinema? Or read? Or eat? Or watch the telly? Or even go on the internet?'

'There are lots of films on the internet these days,' said Dermot, 'Which is very helpful when the fucking TV is so useless. Nothing but the X Factor and fucking Fair City.'

'Ah, I like my bit of Corrie,' said Maggie fondly.

'There you go!' said Mr. Graves, 'There's always the internet when the telly fails. And it also makes sense when the cinema is so expensive. Like everything really. If I may make a grand statement, downloading is only an extension of the freeloading instigated by our friend Conan here.'

'Ah now, but downloading is of dubious legality,' said Conan Kelly, unheard.

'There's a great website called Putlocker which I recommend highly,' said Dermot.

'I'm sure it's great,' said Mr Graves with some steel, keen to keep on course, 'But I suppose a point I might make is that we can't always be looking at screens in the evenings. We need to get out, have a bit of fresh air, get exercise! But, for that matter, that needn't always mean go to the pub.'

'Sure it's too expensive too!' Dermot said petulantly, 'Just why these gigs are such a godsend. Dunno where I'd be without Conan's list. Gives you something decent to look forward to.'

'True, these events are decent. They are free. They are very instructive sometimes, especially if one arrives for the speeches and you don't just pop up at the afters. I'm not in any way disputing that. But a change of habits is good sometimes. That's all I'm saying. For instance, when were any of you last in the countryside? When did you get a chance to cut loose and leave the city?'

'Oh, not for yonks,' said Maggie Magee wistfully.

'Saw the sea last summer,' said Dermot vaguely.

'Kjjhl,' said Conan Kelly, detaching a chip of snot from his nose.

'Dunno now,' said Vernon Crumb glumly.

'Isn't it a crying shame!' said Mr Graves, 'I'm a country man myself by birth, as some of you may know, and it would kill me to be always stuck in the city night and day. A bit of country air really does the soul some good. Just think of it – a woodlands retreat, to live like a hermit and get back in touch with nature. To wake up to the sound of bird-song and not the fecking traffic.'

Vernon Crumb looked thoughtful. While insightful Maggie started to see where Martin was heading with this tenuous thread, and she silently applauded the subtlety of his strategy.

'Just think,' said Mr Graves dreamily, 'To be as St Kevin in Glen-dalough...'

'Bah!' Dermot snorted, 'They have loads of them fucking hippie retreats going on all over the place. Full of wankers pretending to be mystical with their jingling bells. Not for me.'

'No, not for you, Dermot,' Mr Graves conceded, 'You're something of a young man still and you couldn't live without the bright lights and the noise and the variety. But when you get to my age, it's a real soother. For instance, my brother-in-law has a country house out in Kildare, small little place, very cosy, big thick stone walls, high trees all around, and the nearest village is half an hour away. It's a lovely place but he doesn't often get a chance to go down since he's so busy. But he sometimes lets me stay there since I'm a light guest and don't have a family attached with a lot of bawling brats making a mess all over the place. Great chance to escape when the going gets rough.'

'Getsh worsh before it getsh better,' Vernon Crumb remarked softly.

'And in fact, now that I think about it,' said Mr. Graves, raising eyes to the ceiling and stroking his chin (a flawless impression of a sudden inspiration, giving an air of spontaneity to the carefully contrived scheme he had hatched overnight), 'such a retreat could be exactly what ...'

He stopped, wary of over-egging the pudding before it baked. They waited, ever more eager.

'What what?' cried eager Maggie Magee, leaning forward. 'Come out with it, Martin!'

'Yeah man,' Dermot chipped in, 'Don't leave us hanging here!'

'Well,' said Mr Graves with a slow smile, '… it struck me just now that such an escape could do wonders for our friend Vernon here. Place to put his feet up and really convalesce. Hm?'

In the succeeding silence that followed, he turned to each of them in turn with encouraging eyes, looking lastly upon the bedridden Vernon, whose rasher face wavered between wary and keen.

'What d'you think, Mr Crumb?' said Mr Graves. 'I've got a set of keys right here. Just need to put the word in to my brother-in-law and the place is all yours. And I'm sure you'd be a good houseguest. If you play your cards right, why, you could stay indefinitely. What d'you say?'

'O Vernon!' Maggie Magee cooed, turning to her lover and nudging his ribs, 'It'd be the making of ye!'

'Not to be sniffed at,' Dermot sniffed, feeling thirsty, 'If you can stand the fucking solitude …'

Vernon Crumb considered. Mr Graves took out a set of keys from his pockets and jangled them enticingly in front of his nose, laughingly dropping them before him on the bedspread. Vernon Crumb looked at them, one short, one long, silver and golden, well cut, ready to lock and unlock.

'I can drive you up myself as soon as it's arranged,' Mr Graves added, a droll eyebrow uplifted. 'Think of it as a package holiday without the ticket price attached.'

'Once Dermot's cousin has fixed his teeth, of course,' said Maggie Magee seriously.

'Can be easily done,' Dermot murmured, scratching an armpit.

'First things first,' said Mr Graves.

'Jghtd bhft,' Conan Kelly joked. Everybody laughed.

Vernon Crumb thought. Everybody waited. And then, with ceremony, with deliberation, the invalid stretched out a shaking arm and scooped up the keys deposited on his bedspread. He held them to his ear and listened to their jingle as he gently shook them. And then he smiled and nodded.

'Soundsh good to me,' he whispered.

Everybody applauded and the mood was merry. To clinch the deal and tentatively celebrate this sagacious course of action, expectant Dermot produced a hip flask and offered its contents to the company. This motion was initially deplored until finally they agreed that a final sip would do Mr Crumb no harm – so long as his measure was expressly compounded more of tea than whiskey. No harm done, mature Mr Graves conceded, rubbing his palms.

'Sure isn't it medicinal anyway,' Conan Kelly muttered. But nobody heard him.

Dermot was as good as his word; his dentist cousin, a lovely lad who often gave to charity, offered a knockdown bargain price that was well within their price range: and in any case, they all chipped in together for the toothy cause, so firm were they in one. Within a week, Vernon Crumb was freshly equipped with a shining new set of polished dentures that lent a sparkle to his smile, and indeed he smiled more often as a consequence. Maggie bought him a new suit, so loving and tender a soul she was, and she did so want him to look his best now that a new leaf was being turned over, and she even went and supplied him with some sturdy wellington boots for walking the mucky boggy roads.

And meanwhile Mr Graves held a careful consultation with his cousin, a banker who was frequently abroad in order to avoid the domestic turmoil it was his partial shame to cause, an incompetent banker who was nonetheless of a kindly disposition at heart, who, after some demurrals, agreed in the end to generously allow his neglected country property to be occupied by an eccentric friend-of-a-relative-by-marriage. Mr Graves encouraged him to think of it as a housesitting exercise – for heaven knows, the place might freeze or fall apart if it was left unattended all the lengthy year long – someone had to be there to sweep the cobwebs and turn on the heat at least, lightweight tasks well within Crumb's capabilities. This angle won the banker over.

And when all was settled and the time was right, Mr Graves acted as chauffeur, pulling up his Lexus at Long Lane and honking his horn to spur on the departing resident, who came ambling out with a lopsided grin, dragging his stroller bag and sack of groceries while fending off the kisses and last minute suggestions of Maggie Magee (who swore to keep a watchful eye on his bedsit in the interim, secretly resolving to give his kip a makeover), dumping his belongings in the boot and hopping inside by the driver's side, waving a last goodbye to his college sweetheart as the car beeped and spluttered and tore away down the lane toward the promise of the west. (Conan Kelly and Dermot O'Connor failed to emerge to wave farewell, for they were boozily incumbent within, having cheekily polished off the contents of reformed Vernon Crumb's capacious cabinet.)

Within an hour of leaving Dublin, they pulled up outside the countryside sanctuary Mr Graves had promised. The Kildare residence was a modest lodge on the corner of a vast estate where horses and cows were reared and milked, the former dwelling of a lonely gatekeeper or sentry in centuries past – the older section was some two hundred years old, consisting of a cosy study complete with erratic internet access, and a chilly kitchen topped off by an antique chimney-pot bedecked with carved vines and stony garlands, with a fine and ravishing view of a nearby roadside river whose constant gush was soothing, and the modern extension entailed a bathroom and a bedroom as well as a baby's room (the one area out of bounds to the caretaker, Mr Graves carefully informed heedful Vernon), and all was surrounded by a large and airy garden enclosed by a high and imposing wall, shutting out the world and preserving the peace. And Vernon Crumb beheld it all and was enthralled, wandering around the garden and admiring the decorative well, breathing the air and blissfully stretching his arms as his saviour Graves filled his fridge and stocked his shelves. And Graves clapped his hands, and announced that he would leave him to it.

As he watched the car speed away, Mr Vernon Crumb briefly regretted the course of action he had taken, and suddenly felt that he had been set up – thoughts of all the receptions he was missing flooded him of a sudden – should have stocked up on booze before coming here – might make the long nights more cheerful – feeling desperate, he searched the house just in case a dusty bottle had been left by accident – but the place was dry as bone. He contemplated the thirty-minute walk to the village where presumably there would be the relief of an off-licence – but then was appalled by the thought of the long walk back with laden arms. And so he sulked and mourned.

But soon, having no alternative, he dismissed his futile woes. He settled in. He ate an apple. He sat at the patio table in the garden and drank a cup of tea. He watched the sun's rays and the shadows that were cast. He looked up at the clouds and admired their breezy passage overhead and the dots of flocks who passed and flew. He listened to the songs of birds and the faraway barking of hounds. He threw crumbs to the robins and smiled upon the frogs. He enjoyed the scuttle of the squirrels who swung from the swaying boughs, hotly disputing their claims on the nuts. He listened to the rustling leaves and the nearby gush of the gurgling stream. He cooked a modest dinner of eggs and beans and felt full. He took a book from the shelves and read deep into the night. And he slept well that night and did not dream. In later ensuing days he walked the winding roads where puddles were scattered, surveying the hilly vistas graced by the light. He saw scarcely anyone, save an occasional jogger, and he scarcely missed society.

For recreation, he read every book that filled the shelves, of which there were many, and he had all the time in the world to read them. Sometime later, feeling curious, he checked his email (hating the grinding sound of the awaking laptop that was an obscene stain upon the silence), and found it loaded with some hundred messages all from Conan Kelly, announcing this and that. Without a moment's thought, he deleted the lot and smiled.

A month later and they had not heard from him. Anxious, they drove down just to check up. Only to find him lying dead in his bed, a hand-made crucifix clutched in his cold hands. So if nobody could quite tell where Mr Vernon Crumb had come from, they could certainly tell where he had arrived.

The Dead

Peter Murphy

Lily, the caretaker's daughter, was literally run off her feet.

T was three days I hid out in the caves of the Isle of Hell, resting my bones by day, waiting all the night for sign of e'er a smugglers' boat. Godspelt truth that wait was tedious in the extreme but at last my luck cem good: as dusk was descending on the third long day I spied a wee motorboat coursing through the sound, its engine mufflered to a drone. Bootleggers to be sure. I watched from among the rocks while them snakey smugglers put ashore and rolled their petern drums up the slope towards their lair, and no sooner were they out of sight ner I legged it for the boat.

The little outboard motor was still ticking hot: a tug upon the cord and up she fired. Ne'er had I handled such a vessel in my life but it required no great skill, I mane to say a chile could of operated such a craft. In a jiffy I had her turned about and off we sped, the smugglers' curses swallied by the wind as the nose of that wee skiff rose to meet the grey waves on the surge. I kep a sure hand upon the tiller and navigated by the stars and prayed that there be fuel enough to freight me across the sound.

Mebbe half an hour had passed afore I glimpsed the hump of ole Hyberny's shore. Harberward I steered, assisted by the wind and tide, and when I was a spit from port I throttled down and let the current take us in. Then I lept into the shallas and hauled that tub ashore and fate it must of appeared to any watching soul as though some creetcher from the dawn of man was emerging from the waves, his ark in tow.

I looped the mooring rope around a pylon on the wharf and cast my eyes about. Them harber walls was coated in slimey vines of seaweed and crusted ore with barnacles and shells. Sliddery steps ascended to the bulwark rims, and as I gained the flood-walls' ramparts it was foremost in my thoughts that I had not set foot on ole Hyberny's soil sinst I was a babe.

But there was reckernoitern to be done, so without delay I venchered forth upon the road. Presently I cem upon the outskirts of a town whose name resisted all decipherment – the lettering on the sign was painted out in keeping with the rebels' habit of defacing signposts in the regions for to send milisha men astray.

Into that town I went, and soon I cem upon a busy thoroughfare and lo the goings on ye nebber seen the like. Many gadabouts was public drunk, chaps puking and duking it out, lassies urinating in the common street. Rubbidge everywhere, cans and broken glass and a lady's shoe with a pointy heel – I mane to say what class of lass goes out with both her shoes upon her feet and goes home with only one?

Says I, you'd best be canny hereabouts me lad. I did not dally nor delay but kept into the shaddas creeping quietly like a sly ole creetcher of the night, a badger or a rat. My guts was grumbling something chronic for I had scarcely et a scrap in three long days essep for berries and sloes and such. I supped water from a horse's troff outside a tavern called The Tubs O'Blood but this hardly satisfied my belly's want. From within that public house there cem much chatter and hubbub. I didn't have a penny in my pockets but figgered with a bit of luck the boss-man might have jobs he needed done, mebbe kegs lifted or kindling chopped or whatever donkey-work might warrant a hot meal and a cot.

Through them bat-wing doors I stepped. A clatter of rough-looking folk was playing cards and drinking grog and some was sucking wenches' faces. A wee piana played in the corner, keys moving of their own accord like a row of denchers gnashing on the notes. As I med my way towards the bar the room entire went deadly silent even the player piana ceased its rinky-dink. The barman was a burly lad with a walnut head and an expression on his mug as though he'd supped his beer and tasted vinegar.

—We don't serve your sort in here, says he. Go back from whence ye cem.

I did not want a quarrel with these drinking men so back I went into the thoroughfare. The sun was fully down now it was chill and gloomy gone. I proceeded past a livery and a locomotive yard and on the edge of the town I passed a derrick rusted to the core, and as I did a monkey-voice inside my brains advised me I'd be better matched to leave this hostile land and return to the Isle of Hell afore the motor-boat was fecked.

Shut your bake, says I to that jeery monkey, and on I kep.

The yella moon dispensed a jaundiced cast upon the night-time world. I was not long upon the road when I saw a spire on the rise of hill beyond the town. Where there is holy folk there may be charity, says I, and up I traipsed towards the summit of that hill. Soon I cem upon a whitewashed chapel shack among the woods. I allowed the beggarman can't be a fussypot you must take your ease where it occurs, so through them chapel doors I went and took a pew among the church-folk gathered there.

Upon the pulpit stood an oldy lad I will describe him for you now. His whiskers was long and bushy he wore a fine big pointy hat and in his hand he held a shepherd's crook. I figgered by his aparrel he must of bin of priestly caste, mebbe a shaman or a drude. He was harping on at length and godpselt truth he had a fine ole pair of lungs on him, roared so loud ye could not help but heed his words.

—All of youse are in disgruntlement, says he. Yer backs is broke yer larders bare yer bellies think yer throats bin cut. Yer sick and tired of tarrifs and of taxes. Youse all give out about milisha men and governmen and Mammon.

He took a slug of sumpen from a hip flask then resumed his spake.

—Ye think ye all have all suffered but ye haven't seen the half of it. The gods are vexed with us. Why, I'll tell ye why. Ye have constructed graven idols out of moloch-stuff and worshipped false economies. Ye think that clay is all. Ye ask what will ye do with all yer suffern I will tell ye: Offer it up! Render unto Caesar. No bidness o' yourn whether the Caesar passes it back ner puts it in his pocket. What matters is yer suffern that is the only currency the gods abide. Divest yer cells of finery. Ye cannot get to heaven if yer all weighed down with moloch-stuff.

A penny-plate was going round now folk was rummaging in their pockets.

—Offer it up! says the drude again and he commenced to walk between the pews.

The plate cem round to me I had no odds I passed it on. This did not please the drude lad one little bit.

—Looky here, says he. One among us won't divest his cell of moloch-stuff. A rebel boy from the Isle of Hell no doubt. He bears that stain upon his face and hand. He is the son of Cain who roams the earth and wears the outcast's mark. He is the serpent banished from the garden med to crawl through dirt till judgement day. Unclean! Ye 'bomination! Depart from us ye freek!

By now the congregation was clapping hands and stamping feet and shouting Freek! and suchlike so I allowed I'd best be on my way.

—Bad cess to lot of ye, says I, hastening from the church and down the hill. Sorely aggrieved I was. Barely half a night in ole Hybern and already I had bin ridiculed and put upon the road like a leper or a thief. My feet was tired from tramping and I missed my home upon the Isle o' Hell. Weary to the core I was but still I would not take my ease until I'd put that chapel on the hill behind me, and so I kep upon the road.

Twas after midnight I suspect afore I cem upon a settlement named Bargytown-On-Sea. Godspelt truth it seemed a very blighted spot, not a light by which to navigate nor a tavern at which to sup, and I might of kep upon my way and ne'er stopped only I spied a stalk of flame a-flickern in the darkness on the harber side of town.

What was that light I'll tell ye now twas a bonfire planted in a tar-barrel on a patch of waste ground near the wharf, around which was gathered a parcel of tramps warming their cells and sucking from cans and naggins and keeping one another company.

Straight off I reckernised their sort as the class of jackdaw folk what got by collecting scrap and bartering it to the any-old-iron man, or what brought recyclables to the mobile mart for to be traded in exchange for cans of brew. Clouds of glowing ash rose from the fire and settled in their hair like bits of burning snow, but they did not seem to notice or to mind – fate it was as though they had no nerves at all.

—G'mora to ye men, says I, saluting this assembly, adding – Ladies too – when I saw that some among their number was of the fairer sex, though ye hardly would of known from their attire. Six in number they was, gaunt and ragged and a starvation to barbers. They was queer of eye and waxen skinned with faces like death-masks, but I could not walk another step so I elected I would stop with them a spell until the weariness had departed from my limbs.

No sooner had I sat among their number ner the tallest of them jackdaw folk passed to me a can of brew from which to swig. I allowed twould be unmannerly to refuse and so availed my cell of a sup or two, and as the grog cheered my blood he told me all about the recent happenings in Bargytown-On-Sea.

Now it had come to pass that some weeks previous a squad of bold milisha men from way up norn was dispatched to punish local folk for sheltering rebel collaborators. What did these blaggards do, says you. Says I, they set Bargytown-On-Sea's only library alight and burnt it to the ground. Why the library, says you. I'll tell ye why. Milisha men knows well a library is the root of all insurgency. Iffen ye burn a people's books ye burn their memory, and iffen ye burn their memory ye burn their history, and iffen ye burn their history they are no more ner drones. Says the merceners: Let this be a lesson to the lot of ye for harbern terrorists, and they torched that fine ole library.

According to them jackdaw folk the noise the fire generated was like a thousand breaking bones. Flames licked the sky, a hunnerd devils' tongues. Gouts of smoke rose ore the chimneytops, a thick and evil cloud that billowed to the firmament. Razed to its foundations, every stick of that establishment, plates of glass exploding into smithereens. No fire brigade to hose the flames, not a soul to save the books but for them merry tramps. Into this charnel house they venchered as the fire raged and burned, but alas their efforts was for naught. That library was turned to ash and char and half-burnt furniture and scorched computer hardware leaking wires. A storm of burning paper floated in the the air so thick it appeared as though that edifice of brick and glass was now a massif snowglobe med for the amusement of a chile.

Aye and all them books was cindered essep for one. One last remaining book, blackened beyond reading bar a hunnerd pages odd. This half-burnt book was likely the sole and only volume left in-tack in the town entire, for in them times folk could ill afford storage for bound and printed matter and was obliged to keep all written records saved on drives or memory sticks or discs. When the town's power outed all batteries ran flat and the library was left as sole repository of record, and now that too was gone.

Well them vagrants seized upon this half-burnt book and freighted it to their camp. They was very sad to see the library burnt for it provided shelter in the raw cold months when the junk-monkeys and grog-zombies took ore the harber and the Rockland plain and erected platforms in the trees and terrorised all who venchered in their domain, unchecked since the local cops had gone on strike and the governmen called in contractors known to one and all as Fat Bastards – apes and brutes who would not lift a finger to enforce the law without a bribe. Entire towns was no-go areas now, parks and woodlands overrun with chavvies while good decent folk stayed indoors after dark.

They wormed into their sleeping bags, those merry tramps, pulled tight their coats again the brazen wind and huddled round the barrel like their ancestors did in caves, and they supped from jars or smoked up bowls of croak while the tallest tramp – his name was Doc – began to read in the flickering light, and the soft lap of the waves put music to his recitation.

He was a learned man, the Doc, a teacher once, took much pleasure in them printed words. He read for his gathered pals a tale that told of a party on the feast of the epiphany many years ago, of folk with names like Gabriel and Mary Jane and Lily the caretaker's daughter, Miss Kate and Miss Julia, Gretta and Miss Ivors and Miss Furlong and the drunkard Freddy Malins and his mum.

And O the grub! Diamond-bone sirloins and goose and ham and parsley and spiced beef. Jelly and jam, almonds, raisins, figs, custard, chocolates and sweets – twould put a hunger on any soul. Oranges and apples, sherry and port, three-shilling tea and bottled stout. Puddings, ale and minerals, apple sauce, stuffing and potatoes and a stick of celery, capital for the blood. I groaned at the thought of such a spread, for the belly was dropping out of me with the want of a decent feed. I said as much aloud, but my companions' eyes went blank and uncomprehending at my talk of bodily appetites.

Now the story told of champion dancers and Italian tenors and monks what slept in open coffins. It told of a lass named Gretta Conroy stood in shadow with her ear cocked to a sad ole song, 'The Lass of Aughrim', while her husband Gabriel romanced about the snow that gathered like a shawl upon her shoulders, but soon enough his randiness was doused by her remembrance of a traveller lad named Michael Furey…

And most among them jackdaw folk agreed the writer of the book had caught the ache of it just right – essep for Crazy Mary, who disagreed most vociferously. Did they not agree, says she, that the fella in the book was an awful class of gom, cuckolded by a corpse? *Generous tears*, she jeered, flecks of spit upon her lips as she spoke of love as a delirium, a con.

On she raved about how *virgin worship is first cousin to whore hatred*, and if you scratch the skin of any sentimentalist you'll find a chauvinist, cos it's the *icon* of a woman they're mooning over, not the real thing, for a woman pisses, shits and bleeds just like a man. Worse ner them singers on the satellite wireless, said Crazy Mary, with their ever-fecken veneration of the *she*, some dickless git always bleating about some bird he was trying to get into the knickers of – and most likely once he got her knocked up he'd be using her for a punch-bag.

—*The men that is now is only all palaver and what they can get out of you*, quoted the Doc, and Crazy Mary laughed and said – He got that much right at least.

What made her so very bitter, I wonder now? Had she known the cruelty of milisha men, the violations they committed to break the will of the rebels' women and in so doing break their men? Had her heart bin badly wounded by a cad? No one could tell – there is no insterment to quantify the hurt behind the staring eye.

But now the Doc put forth his counter-argument. Says he, iffen ye go looking for the stuff of human virtue in a work of art ye will be sorely let-down every time. Pick the bones offa man's words like a carrion bird if you so desire, but any story worth its salt can't be esplained so much as felt in the blood and bones. The meaning is in its feeling, says the Doc, self-evident as the sun and enduring as long, revealing more with every reading, the shine of it never fading with the passing of the times. So ye can analyse and criticise all ye like, my girl, but ye must read the story with yer heart and not yer mind.

That's how the Doc spoke, twas very high-faluting, fate. But Crazy Mary would hear none of it.

—Heart me arse and cabbage, she said. The jar has made you soft.

And on it went until the discourse sputtered out and the company fell to snoring one by one. But when the dawn's first beams did pierce the sky the half-burnt book was gone. Crazy Mary had only gone and tossed it in the fire, and behold that book that wouldn't but halfway burn, well in the end it burned just fine.

Now the sun was rising I allowed I must take leave of my companions. I roused the Doc to shake his hand and bid farewell, but as I grasped that claw in mine I felt his skin was deathly cold and knew no living blood could run inside such icy veins. The Doc withdrew his hand I saw no lines upon his palm. I cast my eyes around at the assembly now awake, that mask-like skin, their queer-set eyes, and in those eyes the fear that I might tell: every one of them a ghost.

I turned on my heels and fled. Bolted like a hare I did and ne'er cast my eyes behind until I'd cleared that harber town. And godspelt truth until this day I've ne'er told a soul about the night I spent conversant with the spirits of jackdaw folk burnt in the library in Bargytown-On-Sea. A chill comes ore my bones to think of it, for even as I speak I feel full sure that ye can hear my cockle-shells still ringing with the prating of them vagrant dead.

About the Authors

Thomas Morris's debut story collection, *We Don't Know What We're Doing*, will be published in 2015 by Faber & Faber. He lives in Dublin, where he is editor of *The Stinging Fly*.

Patrick McCabe was born in 1955 in Monaghan. He is the author of several novels, including *The Butcher Boy* (1992), which was shortlisted for the Booker Prize and won the *Irish Times* Irish Literature Prize for Fiction; *The Dead School* (1995), and *Breakfast on Pluto* (1998), which was also shortlisted for the Booker Prize. *The Butcher Boy* and *Breakfast on Pluto* have both been made into motion pictures. His latest novel, *Hello Mr Bones/Goodbye Mr Rat*, was published by Quercus in 2013. Pat is currently working on a book of short stories and writing plays. He is married to the artist Margot Quinn and they have two grown-up daughters.

Mary Morrissy was born and grew up in Dublin. She started writing as a teenager and has written three novels and a collection of short stories. Her short fiction has been anthologised widely. She has spent thirty years as a working journalist on three of Ireland's national dailies. Since 2000 she has taught creative writing both in Ireland and the US and is currently associated with the MA in Creative Writing at UCC. She divides her time between Dublin and Cork.

John Boyne is the author of eight novels for adults and four for young readers, including the international bestsellers *The Boy in the Striped Pyjamas* and *The Absolutist*. His work is published in 46 languages.

Donal Ryan was born in Tipperary in 1976. His first two novels, *The Spinning Heart* and *The Thing About December* are published by The Lilliput Press and Doubleday Ireland. *The Spinning Heart* won the Irish Book of the Year Award, the Guardian First Book Prize, and was long-listed for the Man Booker Prize, while *The Thing about December* was shortlisted for the Irish Novel of the Year award. Donal is married and lives in Castletroy, Co. Limerick with his wife and two children.

Andrew Fox was born in Dublin and lives in New York City. Among his awards are the RTÉ PJ O'Connor Award for radio drama. His first book, a collection of short stories, is forthcoming from Penguin Ireland.

Evelyn Conlon was born in Monaghan. Her earlier novels *Stars in the Daytime* and *A Glassful of Letters* deal variously with social and political dilemmas. Her last novel, *Skin of Dreams*, which was shortlisted for the Irish Novel of the year award, dealt with the profundity surrounding capital punishment, while her current novel *Not the Same Sky* tells the story of the 4000 Famine orphan girls who were shipped to Australia courtesy of the Earl Grey Scheme, on twenty-one ships between 1848 and 1850. An elected member of Aosdána, she has been writer-in-residence in colleges in many countries and at University College Dublin.

Oona Frawley was born in New York City to Irish actor parents. Oona eventually settled in Ireland in 1999 full-time, and completed her PhD (City University of NY) in 2001. Prior to becoming a full-time academic Oona worked in a beer factory, and as a lifeguard, a waitress, an ad copywriter, and as a freelance editor. Oona has taught at UCD, QUB and TCD, and has lectured English at Maynooth since 2008. Her first novel, *Flight*, was published by Tramp Press in 2014.

John Kelly has published several works of fiction, including *Grace Notes & Bad Thoughts* and *The Little Hammer*. His short stories have appeared in various publications and a radio play called *The Pipes* was broadcast in 2013. His novel *From Out of the City* was published by Dalkey Archive Press in 2014. He lives in Dublin, where he works in music and arts broadcasting.

Belinda McKeon was born in Ireland in 1979 and grew up in Co. Longford. Her debut novel, *Solace*, was published in 2011 by Scribner (US) and Picador (UK/Ireland/Australia). It was named a Kirkus Outstanding Debut of 2011 and was named Bord Gáis Energy Irish Book of the Year 2011 at the Irish Book Awards, as well as winning the *Sunday Independent* Best Newcomer award. It also won the 2011 Faber Prize. Her writing has been published in journals including *The Paris Review* and *The Dublin Review*, and has been anthologised in *Fishamble Firsts: New Playwrights* (New Island, 2008) and *New Irish Short Stories* (Faber, 2011). She has also written on the arts for *The Irish Times* for over ten years.

Michèle Forbes is an award-winning theatre, television, and film actress. Born in Belfast, Northern Ireland, her film work includes *Omagh* (BAFTA winner, Best European Film San Sebastian Film Festival, Discovery Award Toronto International Film Festival, Best Actress Monte Carlo) and she has toured worldwide with such productions as *The Great Hunger* and *Dancing at Lughnasa*. She studied literature at Trinity College Dublin and has worked as a literary reviewer for *The Irish Times*. Her short stories have received both the Bryan MacMahon and the Michael McLaverty Awards. She lives near Dalkey, Dublin with her husband and two children. *Ghost Moth* is her first novel.

Paul Murray is the author of the novels *An Evening of Long Goodbyes* and *Skippy Dies*. He lives in Dublin.

Eimear McBride grew up in the west of Ireland and studied acting at Drama Centre London. Her debut novel *A Girl is a Half-formed Thing* took nine years to publish and won the inaugural Goldsmiths Prize.

Elske Rahill graduated from Trinity College Dublin with an M.Phil in Creative Writing and Gender and Women's Studies. As an actor she appeared in the Abbey and Gate theatres. Author of the plays *After Opium* (2003) and *How to be Loved* (2008), she is currently working on a short story collection. Her first novel, *Between Dog and Wolf*, was published by The Lilliput Press in 2013. She lives in France with her partner and their three boys.

Sam Coll grew up alternately in Dublin, Tokyo and Beijing. He did a stint of writing film reviews for *Totally Dublin*. He has acted in numerous plays, one of which went to the Edinburgh Festival in 2012. He is co-founder of the non-profit collective Spoonlight Theatre Company. An excerpt of his debut novel, *The Abode of Fancy*, will be published in *Granta* in Autumn 2014.

Peter Murphy is from Enniscorthy in Co. Wexford. His first novel *John the Revelator* was published in the UK and Ireland by Faber & Faber and in the US by Houghton Mifflin Harcourt, and was nominated for the 2011 IMPAC literary award, and shortlisted for the 2009 Costa Book Awards and the Kerry Group Fiction prize. His second novel, *Shall We Gather at the River* (2013), is published by Faber in Ireland and the UK and as *The River and Enoch O'Reilly* in the US. He is also a founding member of the spoken word/music ensemble The Revelator Orchestra, whose first album *The Sounds of John the Revelator* was released in October 2012.